"Will you

Hamp's voice revealed a fierce desire, but his touch was gentle as he brushed back a lock of hair from Dani's face.

She lifted her hand to stroke his strong jaw. "I want to," she said honestly.

He searched her features, then heaved a sigh. "But you won't." When she started to speak, he stopped her with a short, hard kiss. "You don't have to explain. I know . . . the kids."

Without further conversation they walked up the path until they reached her door. She turned to him then, the expression in her eyes an echo of his frustration. He plunged his free hand into his pocket and jingled the change there to keep from grabbing her.

"On second thought . . ." She smiled softly.

"What?" he asked, hardly daring to hope.

She reached over and tugged the hand out of his pocket. "It would be against all the laws of nature and the species for teenagers to be home before midnight. . . ."

Marion Smith Collins got the writing bug early when she was seven and won an award for her essay on protection of our feathered friends. The thrill of seeing her words in print never faded. She studied journalism in college and while bringing up her two children she wrote features for the local paper, press releases for civic clubs, political advertising—anything to keep her hand in. And then, six years ago, she wrote her first romance . . . and discovered her niche. "I want to do this every day for the rest of my life," she says with conviction.

Marion and her attorney husband of thirty-one years live in Georgia, where Marion was born.

Books by Marion Smith Collins

HARLEQUIN TEMPTATION

63–THIS TIME, THIS MOMENT
86–WITHOUT A HITCH
114–FOR LOVE OR MONEY

Foxy Lady

MARION SMITH COLLINS

Harlequin Books

TORONTO • NEW YORK • LONDON
AMSTERDAM • PARIS • SYDNEY • HAMBURG
STOCKHOLM • ATHENS • TOKYO • MILAN

This book is dedicated to my friends of Georgia
Romance Writers and, in particular, to the four who
have come to be more than friends. Allies and
advocates, chums and confidantes—I wish every
writer had friends like these.
Donna, Nancy, Sandra and Shannon.
We are fa-mi-ly.

Published July 1988

ISBN 0-373-25311-7

1

HAMP LOWELL released the middle button of his sport jacket and spread his arms across the back of the empty seats flanking his own. He crossed one ankle over the opposite knee. Casually he looked around at his fellow passengers, all of whom were waiting for their flight to be called.

Immediately his gaze was intercepted by one of the uniformed flight attendants clustered near the check-in counter. She had taken a quick but thorough inventory of his broad chest and long legs. Then her eyes met his, and her smile was inviting and only slightly obvious.

Allowing himself a tinge of regret, he denied the temptation to respond. His attention moved on. A colorful group, he thought, his gaze now skimming the hundred or so people waiting for the plane. Another woman caught his eye briefly before his view was blocked by a tall figure in the crowd.

Hamp experienced a fleeting impression of familiarity, enough to make him curious. He leaned forward slightly, the action providing him with a glimpse of auburn hair. The blocking figure shifted and he could see clearly again.

No, he didn't know the woman, though her face still seemed familiar. She reminded him of someone, but he couldn't think who. He didn't know any redheads.

She was beautiful in a flamboyant sort of way. Her features were evenly balanced in a heart-shaped face. Her eyes—they appeared to be green, but from this distance he couldn't be sure—were large and spaced wide apart, her nose slightly retroussé, and her lips full and provocative. Her pretty jawline ended in a delicately pointed chin. The bright pink of her slacks and shirt, which should have clashed with her coloring, didn't clash at all. She wasn't tall—about chin height to him, he judged—and her body was exceptional—tiny waist and rib cage, full breasts, long legs.

"They didn't have the *Wall Street Journal* so I got you *GQ* instead."

Hamp forgot about the woman as a smiling young girl flopped into the chair beside him. His expression of distaste was not for her, but for the magazine she held out. "*GQ*? You know I never read that kind of magazine, Sandy."

When he didn't take the magazine she dropped it into his lap, her cornflower blue eyes narrowing, and rested her neck against his arm. "Well, you should. Look around you. Do you see any other men here wearing a coat and tie? I have news for you, Hampton Serling Lowell III. The yuppie look is out." She shook her head on a sigh.

Fascinated, Hamp noted that the blond spiky strands of her hair were not disturbed by the movement of her head. He wondered what kept them that way. "I'm a traditionalist, not a yuppie," he protested lightly.

"Whatever," she conceded with an exasperated grin. "We're supposed to be on vacation, but you're dressed like you're ready to teach a class in Pacific history."

Hamp let his hand rest lightly and briefly on her shoulder. He felt a rush of affection for the lovely young thing and gratitude that she seemed to be in an exceptionally good mood. If they could sustain the lighthearted attitude, this vacation—their first together—would be a success. He grinned back at his diminutive daughter. "Your old dad's pretty bad, huh?"

"Bad means good," she corrected automatically, while pretending to appraise him. "No, you're not bad at all. You're a handsome man for your age, Daddy. But you should take advantage of it."

Controlling his urge to laugh, he eyed her dubiously. For his age? Lord, the child made him feel as though thirty-nine was at the edge of senility. Still he supposed he'd asked for it in a way when he'd decided that being a father was more important at this point in her life than being a pal.

"I keep telling you, you need to shake loose," she continued. "Get out of those grandfather rags and into something colorful. The way you look, you might as well be forty years old!"

Hamp tilted his head back and released the laughter. The sound of his pleasure drew several interested looks their way. "Oh, Sandy," he said, "I'm almost there, you know. I'll be forty in August."

Suddenly she sobered, and the effect was like turning off a light behind her blue eyes. She tucked her chin into the loose neck of her sweater. "That's right. Mother would have been thirty-nine in September."

Hamp pulled her close for a quick hug. "Hey, honey. We're making it okay, aren't we?" he asked quietly, gently tilting her face up.

Her smile was an effort, he could tell, but she tried and he blessed her for the attempt. "Yes, Daddy. We're making it okay."

"JUST CALM DOWN, David. I'm absolutely sure the tickets are in here somewhere." An intrusive lock of auburn hair blocked Dani's vision. She hooked the hair behind her ear and commenced to ramble deeper in her oversize tote bag.

The tall young man at her side smiled slightly. "I'm perfectly calm, Mother."

She glanced up to meet the twinkle in his eyes with a smile of her own. "I know you are, dear. You never get upset about anything."

The light from the wide window beside them shifted, shadowing the twinkle. Or was it the light? "David?" she said softly, worrying.

Suddenly the twinkle reappeared, accompanied by a chuckle this time. "I get upset, Mom, just not over things that aren't important—like the tickets I watched you stow in there an hour ago. Do you want me to look?"

Dani ignored the offer; she bent over the bag to hide her disturbed expression from her son. "Here they are." She held them up triumphantly and handed them to the flight attendant, who tore off a section and returned them, this time to David's outstretched hand.

"Maybe you should take charge of these," joked the man. "She seems to be a bit disorganized."

At any other time Dani would have been offended by the man's remark; but then, at any other time she wouldn't have had to search for the tickets. Flying was one of the rare situations in which Danielle Fox found herself nervous and at a loss.

A grinning David took her arm. "I could get to like this," he said. "My tough, efficient mom, reduced to timidity."

"Don't get used to it," she growled with mock fierceness.

As they entered the jetway she caught sight of the young girl she'd noticed earlier entering the newsstand as they were leaving. She was adorable. Blond and diminutive, she was dressed in the latest style as dictated by the mall generation—a short, sage-green skirt and matching oversize cotton sweater, which almost fell off one shoulder.

"There she is, David," Dani whispered to her son. "Isn't she cute? And she's going to Tahiti!"

"Mom." The word was drawled in the put-upon tone that teenagers have been using on their parents since the dawn of time. "This plane continues on to Fiji, you know."

Dani smiled, relenting. "Maybe she's going to Tahiti," she amended.

He spared a glance for the girl before he returned his mother's smile. "Maybe," he agreed. "But she looks pretty young, Mom. She's probably not fifteen yet."

Dani glimpsed the girl's delicate profile as she turned her head to say something to the man who walked beside her. Too young? How could he tell? Her attention was caught by the man. Tall and good-looking, he looked to be in his late thirties. If the girl was too young for David, she was definitely too young for her companion.

"Hey," said David suddenly. "I don't believe it. That's Professor Lowell with the girl."

"The history professor who interviewed you for the scholarship to Stanford?"

His interest spurred, David hurried her along with a hand at her elbow. "Yeah, that's right. He's a great guy. Professor!"

The tall man stopped at the door to the aircraft, looking back. He was obviously surprised and just as obviously pleased at the encounter. "David! Good to see you." Almost on an eye level, the man and the boy shook hands.

"Professor, I'd like you to meet—"

"Sir, your tickets?" interrupted the attendant who stood at the door of the aircraft.

The professor handed them over; David did the same, and they all moved into the first-class cabin. "Professor, I'd like you to meet my mother, Danielle Fox," David said, as though presenting her for the professor's approval.

Dani smiled indulgently at the faux pas. She knew that this man had become something of a hero to her son. And a fatherless boy needed heroes. But when she turned to share an adult smile with the man, she found to her surprise that she was being rather indifferently dismissed.

"How do you do, Mrs. Fox?" he said formally, after a brief glance.

Had Dani only known, Hamp Lowell was hard-pressed not to stare openly, for she was the beautiful redhead he'd watched while they waited to board the plane. Now, in the close, confining space between the seats of the airplane, it was almost impossible to keep from brushing against the body he'd admired so thoroughly.

Hamp touched his tie. David Fox's mother, he thought. Interesting. The scent of her perfume drifted across the narrow space to tease his nostrils. She smelled like something French, clearly sweet and sexy as hell. Quickly he reminded himself that gawking would not fit in with the image he was projecting. He began speaking to David.

However unaccustomed Dani was to being ignored, she felt no rancor, only curiosity. For she was not displeased that Professor Lowell's attention was firmly fixed on David. They talked casually, as acquaintances do when they meet unexpectedly, but there was obvious enjoyment, too, in the meeting. She tuned out their conversation, pleased at the professor's genuine interest in her son. But puzzled, too, as she continued to study the man, studying the boy.

Many years of dealing with the public had sharpened Dani's powers of observation. Initially she noticed his regard was speculative, as though pondering, trying to come to some sort of decision that involved David; but slowly, that expression changed to one of satisfaction. Whatever his thoughts were, he had made up his mind about something and seemed content with his judgment. She wondered about what.

While they continued talking she considered the man himself. The professor wore a tailored sport jacket and tie, which in itself was strange enough on this flight of tourists bound for Papeete, Tahiti. His hair, that shade of brown particularly susceptible to streaking by the sun, was medium length, thick and healthy looking and had been styled by a master hand.

His eyes, behind a pair of no-nonsense tortoiseshell-rimmed glasses, were dark coffee brown and maybe a bit too serious. Light lines at their corners attested either to his love of the sunlight or to laughter. She would bet on the former. As she'd observed earlier, he was good-looking, but not beautifully so. His jaw was too firm, his eyes too deep set for beauty, but he looked . . . enduring, as stable as a rock.

Lowell. She had reason to distrust the name. But while it was a prominent one in Palo Alto, it was not uncommon; and this Lowell had been instrumental in helping her son. She dismissed her reservations with a shrug.

Without warning Professor Lowell's attention switched to her. She was caught studying him. She revised her first impression in the blink of an eye. There was something behind the scholarly image, a suggestion that he might have planned to look that way.

Dani felt a shiver travel up her spine as those dark eyes fixed on her in another kind of speculation. This, while not unfriendly, was not nearly so approving as his perusal of David had been.

She met him look for look. He smiled; the shivering sensation was over almost as soon as it had begun, making her wonder at her own imagination.

"David, Mrs. Fox, this is my daughter, Sandy." He nodded in the direction of the young blonde who had been stowing a large tote bag in the overhead compartment. She dropped her purse on a nearby seat and turned to smile at them. "Hello," she said politely.

David was as indifferent in his response to the introduction of Sandy Lowell as her father had been to her, thought Dani, feeling a surge of frustration. Here was this adorable girl, and David was more interested in talking to the sober, stuffy professor.

Left to themselves the woman and the girl faced each other.

"How do you do, Sandy?"

"I know you," said Sandy, her eyes slowly widening in delight as recognition dawned. "You're Foxy. I saw you on television last month, on that benefit telethon. I think you're great."

"Thank you," said Dani. "You're very kind. I enjoyed doing the show." She hesitated but she couldn't resist asking, "How old are you, Sandy?"

The girl blinked, startled by the question. "I'm sixteen. Are you and your son going to Tahiti?"

"Yes, we are."

"Great. So are we," Sandy added. "Where are you staying?"

"Do you need help in finding your seats?" asked the flight attendant impatiently.

Sandy waved a hand. "This is mine," she told the woman, giving her a self-confident smile.

First class, thought Dani, raising a brow. She swiveled to find a crowd of people collecting behind them and put her hand on her son's arm. "Nice to meet you, Sandy. Professor." She nodded at them both. "David, we have to move on. We're holding up the line."

"What? Oh, sure, Mom. Good to see you, Professor."

"Oh, we'll meet again," said the man.

Dani was aware, if David wasn't, of the determination stamping his tone. Again she wondered what had prompted it.

HAMP LOWELL stretched his long legs and glanced over at his daughter. His smile, as he watched her sleep, was flavored with indulgence. He hoped this trip would be the beginning of a closeness that had so far eluded them.

He sighed deeply, letting his book fall in his lap, and took off his glasses. With his thumb and middle finger he massaged the bridge of his nose.

Sandy could look so guileless when she slept. But when she was awake, it was a different story altogether. By the time she had come to live with him a year ago, her personality had already been formed, and without his help, without any input from her father at all. Her mother had been the dominating influence in her life.

With all due respect to his ex-wife, Miriam, though they only lived on opposite sides of the continent, it might as well have been in two different worlds. His was the world of scholarship and university life, hers the life of a television producer in Manhattan. Rarely had he questioned the wisdom of giving her custody of Sandy. The child had seemed to be progressing well. Her grades were good, if not outstanding, her manners satisfactory. He'd seen her on holidays and in the summer, but those visits had been hurried and carried out with well-mannered dispatch.

And then last year Miriam had been killed in an automobile accident. Her parents, also Manhattanites, had offered to take Sandy so that she wouldn't have to leave either her friends or the environment she knew.

Hamp realized, however, that it was time for him to assume the role of full-time parent. He also loved his daughter deeply and was looking forward to being a real father.

Their holiday visits had always gone well, and though he didn't hope for an immediate melding of minds and affection, he had anticipated no major problems. When his ex-in-laws had seemed relieved, he had put it down to their age. That is, until Sandy had moved into the house in Palo Alto.

There was nothing overtly wrong with their relationship. He wanted to know her better, to help her get over the shock of her mother's death as painlessly as possible. However, at first she had seemed to merely tolerate his existence. For several months, the harder he tried, the more withdrawn she became. Improvement in their relationship had been slow, but he had been patient. Now they got along fairly well, with one notable exception—Rocky, the boy with one earring, a sexual kind of swagger and a knowing gleam in his eye.

Sandy had accused Hamp of taking her on this trip to separate her and Rocky. He'd never yet lied to his daughter and he didn't intend to start, so bracing himself for a scene, he'd admitted it. Strangely, the scene didn't materialize and his admission had seemed to please Sandy. He wondered if he would ever understand her.

Hamp shifted in his seat, settling into a more comfortable position. He glanced at his watch. They'd been on the plane for five hours; two more to go. He replaced his glasses and picked up his book again.

He tried to concentrate, but his mind wasn't on the words in front of him. David Fox. Now there was a fine young man. The glasses came off. Absently he bit at the earpiece—a gesture his students would have identified as an indication of deep thought—and stared into the middle distance.

He had learned quite a lot about David Fox from reviewing the youngster's scholarship application, and he was impressed with everything he'd learned. If only Sandy would show an interest in someone like David—someone who took the world seriously, who studied and worked, and yet was well-rounded and active athletically. He was already making plans to encourage a friendship between them.

To say he'd been surprised to discover that the woman he'd seen in the waiting lounge was David's mother was an understatement. And to discover that he hadn't recognized her as the owner of Foxy's was an even bigger surprise. Foxy's was a nice place, a low-key dinner club that had first-rate music. He'd been there several times, the last when one of his favorite jazz groups out of New York was doing a guest stint. Another time he and his date had danced to romantic ballads sung in Foxy's own husky contralto.

Of course, without heavy stage makeup and sequined gowns, she didn't look old enough to be anyone's mother. And David was nothing like her. The young man had black hair; hers was so red it looked hot to the touch. He had clear blue eyes; hers were enigmatically green and framed with lush dark lashes. Her skin was pale and smooth; her mouth, when she smiled, curved with the disturbing promise of sensuality.

Sensuality? Hell, what was he thinking of?

Mrs. Fox was a hundred and eighty degrees off from the more subdued women he preferred. He favored blondes wearing soft, muted colors, who wore the scent of wild-flowers, spoke in soft, muted tones, and smiled with cool dignity. Most assuredly, Danielle Fox was not that type of woman.

Once again he donned the glasses and picked up his book. Staying away from her shouldn't be a problem. She would attract men like flies swarming to honey.

DANI SHIFTED in her seat, searching for a comfortable position. She looked down at the watch on her wrist, hating the sensation of being strapped into a speeding missile and hurled across the vast Pacific. Two more hours before they'd finally be released from their confinement.

She glanced at her son. David slept so easily. The sleep of the innocent, she thought with a small smile. David was exactly like his father. Eighteen years and thoughts of Davey could still bring a lump to her throat. He shouldn't have died. He was so young, only twenty, two years older than David was now and two years older than she was then.

Davey, you would be so proud of the son you never saw, so very proud. He's brilliant and handsome and kind; and what a hard worker he is. He has a savings account that I envy. Now, if I could just get him to relax a bit....

Sandy Lowell could stir up anyone's calm waters, she reflected.

David stretched beside her, lifting his arms over his head. "You awake, Mom?" he asked sleepily.

"Yes, I'm awake." She paused. "You were wrong, David. She's sixteen."

David's arms fell to the armrests. "Mom," he said patiently. "What are you talking about?"

"The professor's daughter. Sandy Lowell. She's sixteen. You're eighteen. I think that would be a perfectly normal age spread."

"Okay. The professor told me they're staying at the same hotel—"

"They are?" Dani had missed that part of their conversation.

"So I'll get a chance to look her over."

"Look her over? David Fox! I can't believe you'd make such a chauvinistic—" Dani broke off her indignant protest when she saw the gleam of amusement in her son's eyes. Ruefully she joined in his laughter.

"You're so easy to rile," he teased. Then his laughter faded. "How could I possibly be a chauvinist, Mother? All my life I've watched you struggle to earn a living," he said grimly. He raked his fingers through his hair.

Dani watched the gesture, a sign of masculine frustration. She didn't like the expression on her son's face, one that she'd seen too often lately. She didn't like it and she didn't understand it. Did David resent what she did to earn that living? Working in a nightclub, even if she did own the club in question, wasn't a normal everyday pursuit among the other mothers in the PTA. "We've managed pretty well though, haven't we?" she asked softly.

"Yeah." Unbuckling his seat belt, he stood. "Excuse me, Mom. I need to move around some."

WHEN THEY STEPPED OFF the plane at Faaa Airport near Papeete, the heat, absorbed during the day by the tarmac, rose from their feet to engulf them in a transparent cloud. Wearily, Dani followed her son off the plane, down the portable steps. David didn't seem to notice the heat.

A babble of languages, dominated by French, greeted her ear. The line to get through customs was long and curved through the doorway so that the front wasn't even visible to those waiting. A string band played at the bend in the lineup, trying to stir up some enthusiasm in the weary travelers. To the beat of the music, Tahitian dancers moved through the crowd, bestowing flowers and kisses of welcome.

"Welcome to Papeete." A smiling young man slipped a garland of flowers, a *hei* he called it, over her head. She smiled her thanks and lifted the delicate flowers to her nose. They smelled of jasmine—exotic and heady. Suddenly she felt her spirits lift and the weariness slide from her shoulders like a discarded cloak.

Finally they passed through the barrier and collected their luggage. That was when Dani discovered that the first line they had gone through wasn't customs at all. "I can't wait to get to the hotel," she complained good-naturedly to David as they took their places in the second line. "I'm not sure why sitting on a plane for seven hours is more tiring than working a full day, but it is. I'm going to take the first cold shower I can find."

David smiled with the energy and indulgence of the young. "When we get through customs, Mom, you find a place to park yourself and the luggage. I'll locate Le Truck and come back for you."

The travel agent had assured them that Le Truck was a respectable bus that was used for transportation throughout the islands and was perfectly adequate to get them to where they were going. "David, dear, are you implying that I'm in my dotage?" she asked sweetly.

But David wasn't paying attention. "There goes the professor," he said in a strange voice.

Dani turned to follow the direction of his gaze. A long black limousine had pulled up to the curb. The driver touched his cap and took the suitcases from the professor. Sandy was already crawling inside.

"I take it that isn't Le Truck," she observed wryly.

David gave her a smile of shared amusement. "Probably not." He sketched a very formal bow. "Ah, well, *madam*, when I'm rich I'll order you a limousine, too."

"As if I care," Dani said cheerfully, earning herself another one of those enigmatic looks.

THE HOTEL at Maeva Beach was lovely. A quick scan of the huge lobby showed shops, an information counter and plenty of comfortable seating. Music from Polynesian guitars played quietly in the background. Groups of large rattan chairs lined with thick pillows were sequestered from other groups by planters filled with feathered palms and trailing vines. Jutting off the lobby, but not separate from it, was a piano bar, open on three sides to stunning vistas of the sea beyond. Lush bougainvillea dripped magenta blossoms from the roof line.

Their rooms were comfortable, too. Situated on the ground level, below the lobby, they opened directly onto a patio and beyond, a beautifully manicured lawn. The sun was setting and tiny lights hidden in colorful borders of scarlet hibiscus began to flicker. Beyond the grass was the beach, beyond that the sea and a view of the island of Mo-oréa, thirty miles away. Off to their right, surrounded by another low hibiscus hedge was the pool area, deserted now.

David stuck his head out of the sliding glass door to his room. "Hey, Mom. I'm going to look around. You want to meet me somewhere?"

"In the dining room? Give me twenty minutes."

"Perfect. I'm starved."

Now that the traveling was over and they were settled in their rooms Dani felt her energy level rising with the excitement that always accompanied a visit to a new place. She hurried through a cool shower and dressed in a light cotton sundress of pale yellow banded at the waist and hem with tangerine, before replacing the flowered *hei* around her neck.

When she examined her reflection she decided that the new dress was rather artless and not her style at all, so she clasped on large earrings of beaten copper. The matching bracelet, a primitive-looking piece, circled her upper arm. She slipped her feet into high-heeled sandals, ran a brush through her heavy, burnished hair, touched her lashes with mascara, her lips with gloss, and grabbed her purse.

David's hand was raised to knock when she opened the door. Dani fell back, a hand over her tripping heart. "David, you startled me!"

"Sorry, Mom." He spread his hands, palms up. "Hey, you look great!" He smiled, but his tone was reserved.

"Thank you, sir." She met his smile. "I thought you were hungry."

He took her arm to direct her away from the stairs. "I am, but there are two dining rooms. I was afraid you'd go to the wrong one."

"Oh? And which one is that?"

"The one with violin music and fancy prices. I'm not dressed for that."

His grim tone brought her eyes to his face. The travel agent had assured her that the Maeva Beach was a hotel to be comfortable in. David wasn't wearing a coat and tie, but his khaki slacks and white shirt looked fine to her. Wondering what had dampened his enthusiasm, she said lightly, "Then I suppose I'm not, either. Lead me to the other place."

The second dining room wasn't a room at all but a huge, circular, covered patio also on the ground level near the pool. A round buffet of colorful and tempting foods sat beneath the peak of the thatched roof and was surrounded by candlelit tables. "I like this better anyway," she told David.

"Yeah, so do I," he replied, his smile relaxed now.

A hostess led them to a table on the side away from the pool, overlooking the ocean. Offshore the island of Mooréa was now nothing more than a black mass rising from the dark sea, but the contrast of shadows gave the promise of a moon later.

"May I bring you a drink?" asked the hostess, her smile warm and hospitable.

David ordered iced tea. Dani asked for a glass of wine. When the woman returned with their drinks she introduced a young man who stood behind her, beaming at them. "This is Toru. He will be your waiter."

"Please serve yourself from the buffet when you are ready," said the waiter in heavily accented English. "If there is something you don't see that you would like, you have only to ask."

"Thank you." Dani thanked him with a smile. "David, if you're hungry, why don't you go ahead and serve yourself? I want to sit here for a minute."

"Okay, Mom."

The breeze that floated in from the water delivered exotic floral scents along with its own salty tang, and Dani closed her eyes to savor the smells. With a sigh she relaxed against the back of the seat. What a heavenly feeling it was to let all the care and responsibilities seep from her body, to let herself be inundated with the peace and quiet comfort of her surroundings. This was the first vacation she'd had in a long time and she fully intended to savor every minute of it.

"Mrs. Fox?"

The deep voice brought Dani out of her reverie with an unpleasant jolt. Her eyes flew open. The candlelight cast shadows over the strong planes of Hamp Lowell's face.

For a split second she was again caught in the magnetism of that dark gaze. This time, instead of indifference or speculation, she read undisguised appreciation in his eyes. It gave her an obscure pleasure that she refused to explore. He had changed clothes, too, she noticed; but the collar of his shirt was just as smooth, his tie and coat just as formal as before. "Professor?"

"David has asked Sandy and I to share your table. I thought I should check with you first," he said, as though good manners alone prompted him to ask. Already his hand was on the chair.

Behind his glasses that absorbing gaze seemed drawn to her bare shoulders, producing another instinctive shiver in Dani. She thought about refusing. Obviously he was as uncomfortable as she at the prospect of sharing a table. As he waited for her answer, she noted a slight flush above his collar. Short of being rude, she couldn't think of a reason to ask him why he would bother.

Casually she crossed her arms and glanced at the hostess. "Certainly," she said with unruffled calm. "Join us if you like."

Nodding, Hamp took the seat across from her. "I'll have Scotch on the rocks," he said to the woman.

The hostess was back almost immediately with his drink. He took a swallow, set the glass squarely in the center of the tiny cocktail napkin and met her gaze. "Are you pleased with your accommodations, Mrs. Fox?" he finally asked, rather coolly, Dani thought.

When coupled with his precisely knotted tie, the tailored fit of his dark jacket, this very staid, very formal opening conversational gambit disposed of any remaining wariness on Dani's part. Setting aside a subconscious warning that she could be too honest for her own good, her lips curved into a mischievous smile. This man needed to be shaken out of his formality or he wasn't going to enjoy a minute of his vacation. She laughed brightly into his eyes and teased, "Professor Lowell, are you always so stuffy?"

The dark eyes narrowed as the flush rose to his tanned cheeks. "Yes, I suppose I am," he murmured, unmistakably annoyed.

Hoping she hadn't made him really angry—her teasing might come back on David—she apologized. "I'm sorry, I shouldn't have said that. My name is Danielle. Call me Dani, please. Mrs. Fox seems much too conventional." The corners of her mouth lifted in a candid grin as she answered his first question. "Yes, I think the accommodations are adequate, don't you? The Tahitian people are lovely. The weather's nice, too."

He looked away, his lips curved in a rueful smile. Finally he expelled one very dry chortle of resignation and toasted her silently with his drink before taking another swallow. "The flight wasn't too bad, either. Now that we've gotten all that out of the way, Dani, I'm Hamp," he said, meeting her eyes and allowing a genuine smile to grow. "You and my daughter ought to get together. She thinks I'm stuffy, too."

"I'm sorry. The comment was uncalled-for." Lord, that smile was potent, thought Dani. And dangerous, she added, returning his toast uneasily. The way the professor said her name, in that deep, very personal way—she would have been much better off leaving him to his formality. With very little effort Hamp Lowell could rattle her emotions and upset her restful vacation.

"Not completely," he admitted. "I suppose I'm a creature of habit. You know, I thought I recognized you when we were waiting for our flight to be called. Sandy filled me in. I've been to your club several times."

She sipped. The cool wine slid easily down her throat. "Really? I hope you enjoyed yourself."

"Very much," he said. "I've even heard you sing."

She lifted a brow. He must not have been there in quite a while. "I don't sing much anymore unless there's an emergency."

"So I've heard. But why? You have a lovely voice."

"Thank you," she said simply, then she shrugged. "Strangely enough I've discovered that I really prefer being a businesswoman. I'd rather be behind a desk than in a spotlight."

"That's a shame," he murmured. "And a loss for your customers. You are very beautiful and very talented."

His dark eyes held her captive as he spoke. Dani had often been complimented on both her looks and her talent, but never quite so simply or sincerely. The flattering tribute had a peculiar, intimately warming effect on her. "I've been lucky to be able to provide good entertainment." Deliberately she tore her gaze away from his, resting it for a moment on the glass of chilled wine, then scanning the dining area.

"Sandy and David are attacking the buffet," he said when he saw her looking in that direction.

"Teenagers are always hungry, aren't they?" she observed lightly, for lack of anything better to say.

He hesitated before answering her. "I suppose so."

Dani wasn't sure why his answer struck her as odd, but it did. Any of the other single parents she knew would have made some laughing remark about hollow legs or bottomless stomachs. Puzzled, she waited for him to elaborate. When he didn't, she let the subject drop. Her fingers curved around the cool glass; she raised it to her lips. Still confused, she had another thought. Maybe he *wasn't* a single parent; maybe his wife took the responsibility for Sandy.

Her reaction to that idea took her totally by surprise. Why should she be disturbed at the thought that he might be married? Why should it bother her at all? She had nothing in common with this man. He was a teacher—worse, a college professor. She'd married right out of high school. He took limos; she preferred Le Truck. And that was information garnered after exchanging only a few dozen words. Heaven only knew what other differences would crop up if they really got to know each other. "Your wife isn't with you?" she asked casually to hide her confusion.

His dark brows formed a frown. "My wife is dead."

Instant sympathy rose out of her confusion. The devastation of losing a spouse was one she could share, though it had been many years since her beloved Davey had died. "I'm sorry," she said softly, setting her glass down. Leaning forward to prop her elbows on the table between them, she linked her fingers under her chin. "I can understand your pain. My husband has been dead for a long time but I still miss him."

"We were divorced many years ago."

"Oh."

"Sandy has only lived with me for a year, since her mother's death." Each word was uttered reluctantly, as though he were unwilling to speak at all, and his reserved attitude had reasserted itself.

Dani shifted uncomfortably in her chair. She let her hands fall back in her lap. "Sandy seems like a nice child," she offered.

"She is. I'm not complaining, simply explaining why I don't know too much about teenagers."

She chuckled. "Neither does any other parent of one, so don't feel alone in that."

Frowning, he made a noncommittal noise. "I'm learning, but slowly. Dani, I'd like to suggest—" Before he could finish, Sandy and David returned to the table, their plates piled high.

Apparently the topic wasn't one he wanted to discuss in front of the children. It was not the end of all conversation, however. To Dani's surprise talk flowed easily around the table. Over the next hour she learned a lot about the Lowells. She learned that, though he might feel he didn't know her, the man deeply loved his daughter. The love was there in every expression as he watched her. Even when tinged by exasperation over the girl's occasional flippancy, the love was very real and would have been obvious to the most casual observer.

But it was also obvious that it was David with whom he had the most in common, David to whom he turned for recognition when he was explaining his intention to accomplish some work while he was here. "I'm planning to spend most of my time on Huahine, to study the village Levy wrote about in *The Tahitians*. Are you familiar with the work?"

David responded with equal enthusiasm. "Yes, sir, I am. His findings about the effects of the modern world on the island culture are incredible. This trip is my graduation present from my mom," he explained. "I'm hoping to get to some of the other islands myself."

Dani found herself trying to follow their conversation with one ear and listening to the more prosaic interests of a young girl with the other. On yet another level, her thoughts kept straying to inappropriate things such as the graceful strength in Hamp's big hands when he gestured, the sensual curve of his mouth and the contrast of his white teeth to his tanned face when he smiled. The task was giving her a headache.

Finally someone had to pause for breath. Dani glanced at her watch. Into the lull she said, "I'm just about ready for bed."

"Bed?" David looked at her as though she'd said she were going to jump from the roof of the hotel.

"Yes, bed," she answered firmly. "It may be nine o'clock here but at home it's midnight. It's been a long day and I'm really tired."

She wasn't surprised when Hamp nodded. "I'm ready to turn in, too. You don't have to, Sandy." The last was in response to Sandy's groan. He signaled the waiter. "May we have our check, please?"

"David, if you're not ready to go in, why don't you and Sandy walk down to the marina?" Dani suggested. "You can check the schedule for the glass-bottomed-boat cruises."

Hamp smiled broadly. "That's a great idea!"

Pleased that he seemed to approve, Dani, nevertheless, shot him a cautionary glance. *Don't overdo it*, her eyes said.

Sandy and David eyed each other dubiously before agreeing. "I won't be gone long, Mom," said David.

"Don't hurry, dear."

After the youngsters had disappeared, she turned to Hamp. "I hope I didn't misread you. It seemed to me that you wouldn't be against their spending some time with each other."

"I'd be delighted if you have no objections. David is a fine young man—unlike the types that Sandy usually brings home," he said wryly. "He'd be a good influence."

"Sandy would be a good influence on *him*. Sometimes David is almost too fine, I'm afraid."

Hamp was surprised by the remark, but he hid his feelings as the waiter placed their checks on the table. Though he reached for both of them, Dani was faster. "Let me," he offered. "We intruded on your dinner."

"Don't be silly," she countered and signed the check with her name and room number.

Hamp's brow lifted and his lips tightened to a line, but he didn't argue as he took the pen and signed his own check. He wasn't accustomed to having a female reject his offer to pay for a meal and he certainly wasn't accustomed to being called silly. He realized, as he studied her more closely, that he was going to have to revise his opinion of this woman. Clearly Danielle Fox was her own woman, not simply beautiful and talented but independent and self-sufficient, as well. Too much so in his opinion. Though he wasn't fond of clinging vines, he liked to see a little bit of vulnerability in his women.

Her smile, when she handed the check to the waiter, was warm and contagious. He recalled the enthusiastic response of the audience in the club when she sang that night, long ago. Now he could imagine taxi drivers and doormen falling all over themselves to please her for a glimpse of that dazzling smile. Was she aware of its power?

Sure she was.

And himself? He found suddenly and surprisingly that he would like to have the warmth from her smile directed toward him. The intensity of that wish disturbed him and he immediately put it out of his mind. He'd walk her quickly to her room, say good-night and leave. Period.

But when they left the table and the restaurant, he forgot to hurry. The tropical night was too perfect to rush. They wandered without direction under the coconut palms, toward the main entrance of the hotel. The promise of a moon had been fulfilled and now cast silver streaks among the shadows.

A door opened. Music and laughter drifted down from a nightclub on the lobby level, breaking the spell. The door closed again, shutting off the sound.

He wrestled with himself and lost. "Would you like to go up for an after-dinner drink?" he asked.

She finally smiled at him then, but it was only half-power. Her expression was friendly and open, nothing there to respond to. He argued away his disappointment. Why the hell should a certain kind of smile make any difference?

"Thanks, no. I really meant it when I said I'm tired."

"Another time, perhaps."

"Perhaps," she agreed noncommittally.

Hamp sought another subject. He was still puzzled by her earlier remark. "I'm confused, Dani, by what you meant when you said David was too fine. From what I know of him, he's intelligent, well-rounded and responsible. I would think he's everything a parent could want."

She hooked the fingers of both hands along the bottom edge of her envelope purse and held it loosely in front of her. "Don't mistake me. I'm grateful that David has those qualities. I love him very much, and I'm proud of him. Lately there's been something . . ." She let the sentence trail off unfinished and shook her head. "I only wish he could loosen up a bit. I'd hoped that after he got the Stanford scholarship—" She turned to look at him. "By the way, I understand we're indebted to you for that."

"No need to feel indebted." He shrugged. "David was far and away the most qualified of the applicants."

"Because he spends all his free time studying." Dani couldn't help the sigh that escaped.

"Forgive my curiosity, but you said your husband died a number of years ago?"

"Yes, before David was born."

"Your family?"

"I have none." She didn't explain about the grandparents who had reared her from the time she was six. A couple who had lived quietly, they'd also died quietly soon after she was married, as though once they'd fulfilled their responsibility, they could let go.

Hamp looked at her for a long moment. When he spoke, his words came out slowly, almost unwillingly. "To bring up such an exceptional son alone you must be exceptional yourself. It has to have been hard on you."

Pleased by the compliment though wondering a bit at the way it was delivered, she laughed under her breath, remembering those years and being glad that the memory could bring laughter rather than tears. "It was a character-building experience," she said lightly. "But David has always taken on responsibilities beyond what was necessary. He had his first part-time job when he was nine." Her smile tilted. "I've worried ever since that he's missing out on so many things."

"I doubt that Sandy has missed out on a thing," said Hamp fiercely, releasing the button of his jacket and plunging his fists into the pockets of his slacks. His eyes were on the path before them. "You don't know how lucky you are," he added almost as though he were speaking to himself.

The action bared his white shirt, emphasizing his flat midsection and long powerful legs, and reminding Dani of those moments of awareness in the restaurant. She thought for a minute before speaking again. "They are such opposites, they probably would be good for each other," she said quietly, bringing her purse to her breast now, holding it as a shield.

Hamp considered her profile in the dim light of the early moon. She was lovely, her features exquisite and finely drawn. "Did I hear an implied 'but' in there someplace?"

She smiled, but kept her eyes on the ground. "You're very quick. The truth is. . . ."

The past month—the past year—had been hectic at the club. Her business was growing faster than she could ever have anticipated. She needed this time away to rest and do absolutely nothing. She needed to sleep late, to go without makeup, to walk the beach and soak herself in sunshine and seawater. She didn't need to become involved with a man at all, and especially not one of such strong masculine appeal.

He was waiting for her to go on. She decided to be completely honest. "The truth is, Hamp, this trip is a rest for me as well as being David's graduation present. I'd love for the children to spend some time together. But I'm not interested in making this vacation into a foursome," she added quickly, before she could change her mind.

She walked beside him along the corridor that led to her room. Had she offended him? After a long pause, she risked a glance at his profile. He was smiling as he met her eyes. The relief in his expression was evident—and slightly insulting—though Dani couldn't come up with an explanation as to why it should affect her that way.

"I agree," he declared, too heartily even for his own ears. But her honesty was refreshing and he responded to it eagerly even as he tried to ignore the soft-looking skin of her bare shoulders. "I just didn't quite know how to put it to you without sounding uncivil."

They had reached her door. She let out a breath that she hadn't been aware she was holding. One hand dropped to her side, keeping a grip on her purse. She extended her other hand. "You're a very nice man, Professor. I think I'd like to have you for a friend. Thank you for understanding." He took the hand and held it; Dani caught her breath at the contact.

"On the contrary, thank *you*. I think I'd like you for a friend, too, Dani Fox."

"We have an agreement, then," she said, pleased that her response to his warm fingers wasn't noticeable in her even reply.

"I suppose we'll see each other around the hotel. Good night, Dani."

"Good night, Hamp."

2

HAMP LAY stretched out on the bed in his shirt sleeves, his fingers laced together beneath his head, his long legs crossed at the ankles. His mouth curved into a smile of satisfaction.

Dani Fox was a diplomatic woman and a perceptive one, as well, endorsing his plan for Sandy to spend time with David, while agreeing that they shouldn't make this a foursome. To his own surprise he'd meant it when he said he'd like to have her for a friend.

He'd planned the trip to Tahiti as a vacation with his daughter, during which he hoped to get some work done. He had several meetings scheduled and didn't want or need diversions of any other kind—no matter how attractive those diversions might be. He quickly amended that thought. He wouldn't mind sharing his work on Pacific history with a scholar of David's caliber; he was a unique and brilliant young man.

What a rare thrill it was when a teacher found a kid like that. He might even ask David to go along tomorrow when he flew to Huahine. Hamp had made arrangements with a local pilot to fly him and Sandy out in the morning, just for the day, to look around and appraise the situation. Later in the week, after Sandy had sampled the sophistication of Papeete, they would move to a hotel on the other island.

But if he took David with them tomorrow, Dani would be left completely alone. He could invite her to go along, too; except she'd made it clear that she didn't want to be with him. She hadn't actually phrased it that way, but the meaning was close enough. She didn't want a foursome? Fine.

Toeing off his tasseled slip-ons, he frowned at the ceiling. That was fine with him. Despite his awareness of her tonight—an awareness that must have been obvious to her—he was hardly a ravenous celibate ready to pounce on the first available woman. Even one as sexy as she.

His earlier satisfaction forgotten, he drew his brows together in a scowl, and the gleam in his eyes intensified. Now that he thought about it, her withdrawal provoked him. Why was the woman so determined to be standoffish?

Hamp was intelligent enough to recognize the quick and obvious metamorphosis of his reasoning, and honest enough to admit that it was a juvenile way for a grown man to respond. Put plainly, his growing attraction to Danielle Fox fed on her indifference.

Normally he exercised fairly good judgment, but this was crazy! He swung his legs off the bed and sat up, resting his elbows on his knees, trying to rationalize the sudden about-face. He always conducted his relationships the same way he conducted his historical research—with initial skepticism and careful analysis, making sure that the women he dated knew that his life centered on his work and, now, his daughter.

Many years ago the football hero and the beauty queen had married the day after graduation, believing that was all it took, believing the romantic propaganda of an effortless happily-ever-after affinity. Before their marriage, both he and Miriam had sailed through their young lives never having encountered the obstacles faced by other adolescents. At twenty-two they were so immature, so untried and untested, that they had entered into marriage with no idea what it would demand of them. They'd learned, too late,

that a good partnership took more than they were willing
or even able to give at that age.

Burying his pride he had to admit that he had been hurt
more deeply than Miriam. Therefore, since his divorce, he'd
made sure that his head always ruled his heart. Knowing
he'd never be able to tolerate marriage again, he had carved
out a set of rules for himself. Rule number one was to avoid
entanglements, and he had sought out women who felt the
same way. Fortunately—in this day and age—there were
plenty who felt as he did.

Now that Sandy was living with him he'd had to make
certain adjustments, but he'd always behaved discreetly, so
the changes had caused no real hardship. For years his sex
life had been just as he liked it—meeting a need in a satisfying way, but not intruding too deeply into his emotions.
He'd learned his lesson. He didn't intend to leave himself
open to the pain of a rupture in his life again.

However, it was becoming a bit of a strain to keep up the
carefully conservative image he'd decided upon when
Sandy had come to live with him. One of the first things he'd
learned about his daughter was that she was growing up too
quickly. Maybe all kids gave that impression these days, but
when his own child was involved it bothered him. Stability
and traditionalism—a particularly conventional parent
lurking in the background of her life—might slow her down
a bit. If she thought of him as a creature out of the Dark
Ages, so be it.

Maybe it was time to loosen the restraints he held on
himself, relax a bit. Not completely; just a bit. His thoughts
returned to Dani. He'd still like to know why she was so determined to keep her distance. He would have sworn, at
first, that there had been something in her eyes. . . .

One hand flat on his knee, he tugged at the knot of his tie
with the other. After a minute he went to work on the but-

tons of his shirt. Contrarily, now that they had agreed not to spend time together, he found himself extremely disappointed. Intellectually he might understand the reasons for his reaction, but that didn't make it any easier to accept.

He stripped off his shirt, balled it up and flung it into the corner. What the hell was wrong with him tonight? He wasn't interested in pursuing the flamboyant redhead, was he? He stood and crossed to pick up the shirt, folding and stowing it in a compartment of his suitcase. It was a crying shame Dani Fox wasn't more like her son.

WHEN HE STEPPED out of the shower ten minutes later, the frown was still in place and his phone was ringing. Water dripping from his large frame, he hurried into the bedroom to answer.

"Hi, Daddy. I just thought I'd let you know I'm in for the night. Were you asleep?"

The frown cleared from his brow. The muscles in his jaw relaxed. With a broad hand he wiped the moisture from his face. "I was in the shower. Thanks for calling, honey. Did you have fun?"

"Umh-hm, it was okay," she said in a distracted voice. "David's so serious, though. It's a shame he's not more like his mother."

Hamp restrained the comment that rose to his lips. "Yes, well . . . I'll see you in the morning, sweetheart."

DANI SAT UP in bed, flung off the sheet, lifted her hair from her neck and sank back against the pillow, letting the long auburn curls fan out around her head. She'd been tossing in bed for an hour; she couldn't get comfortable. David had come in a few minutes ago. She'd heard him moving around in the next room. Now, beyond the wall, all was silent again.

Her thoughts strayed again to Hamp Lowell, as they'd had a maddening tendency to do ever since she'd gone to bed. She hadn't reacted so strongly to a man in a long, long time, if ever.

Restlessly she shifted. She sent her eyes roaming through the colorless shadows, in an attempt to divert her thoughts toward another channel. But they were not so easily diverted.

Underneath the reserved demeanor, behind the glasses and the conservative clothing, he was the kind of man women responded to—one had only to look twice into those dark, promising eyes, listen to that deep, smoky voice....

Punching her pillow, she rolled to her side. Features of the darkened room were barely defined by a thin shaft of moonlight from the crack she'd left in the draperies. She'd have thought a hotel in Tahiti would offer something more original than standard contemporary hotel decor—king-size bed, dresser with mirror, television set, chair and table. Comfortable but unimaginative, she pronounced, then she chided herself. There was nothing wrong with the room.

Except that it was quiet . . . too quiet. On her bureau at home sat a mantel clock that had belonged to Davey's grandmother. It ticked loudly, like any self-respecting clock should. She missed the sound.

That was the problem; that was why she couldn't sleep. It had nothing to do with the professor. Absolutely nothing. So he was gorgeous, so what? She'd said no many times to many more gorgeous men.

The first few years of her widowhood had been devoted to survival. Davey's death had left her desolate and completely alone with a child to provide for, but even during her most desperate hours, she'd never been tempted to look for a man simply to share her burden. She was young and healthy and capable of looking after herself.

She had loved Davey Fox since they were children, growing up across the street from each other. The idea of loving another man just didn't occur to her.

Over the years she'd had a number of opportunities for what might have been successful relationships. But somehow the opportunities never coincided with favorable periods in her life. Either her help had quit at the club and she was ears deep in work, or she'd had to stretch her budget too tightly to accommodate baby-sitters.

She smiled, remembering Richard Nicholson. Richard had immediately perceived her profound love for her son and had played upon it, taking them to the zoo, the beach, anywhere that David could be included. For a few short weeks they had almost been like a family group. Then David had brought a magnificent case of chicken pox home from school and given it to both her and Richard.

There is something very romance-killing about chicken pox. Richard had been transferred to Omaha soon after that. She had a sneaking suspicion that he'd requested it.

As she lay there staring at the ceiling, Dani tried to summon regret for the aborted relationship with Richard, but somehow she couldn't. Had she been looking for someone to marry, he would have been suitable. They could have built a good life together. But even before the chicken-pox episode, she'd realized that there was no magic between them.

Magic? Good Lord, she couldn't believe she'd even thought the word. As of her last birthday she was closer to forty than thirty. Magic was for the young. Unbidden the image of Hamp Lowell rose in her mind. She shoved it aside.

The conversation over the dinner table and their discussion of their children had quickly washed away any stereotyping she might have done when she first met him. The image of conservative teacher and involved parent was true enough, but she had an idea that there were many more layers to Hamp Lowell's personality. She couldn't help wondering if he was trying to be the kind of father he thought Sandy needed. Curious as she was, though, she knew she shouldn't ignore the risk of investigating those layers.

Muttering, she bounded out of bed and crossed to her suitcase, where she dug into a side pocket for the small travel clock she'd packed there. She set and wound it and placed it on the table beside her bed. The ticking sound was faint but audible. With a deep sigh of relief she closed her eyes and slept.

HAMP HEARD the sound of his daughter's laughter before he saw her. Dani, David and Sandy were seated at a table for four under the thatched roof of the outdoor dining room where they'd eaten last night. This morning, however, they were at poolside and their wet suits suggested that they had already been swimming. He scoffed under his breath—so much for not making this a foursome.

Despite last night's resolve, his gaze was drawn unwillingly to Dani. She was talking animatedly to a young Polynesian woman who had a naked baby straddling her hip. There were at least three other men loitering in the background of the scene, their attention fixed on Dani Fox. Like flies to honey, he reminded himself.

As he watched he was struck once again by her graceful gestures and her vitality. This morning her hair was piled carelessly on top of her head, revealing an unexpectedly vulnerable nape. She wore a sleek, one-piece white bathing suit cut high on the leg and straight across her breasts. He'd always found one-piece suits far sexier than the brief bikini style his daughter wore. Over the suit and clinging to her skin in the places where her body was still wet, she had on a sheer cotton cover-up made like an oversize man's shirt with a tailored collar, rolled sleeves and curved shirttails.

He wondered what she would look like dressed in *his* shirt and nothing else. Impatient with himself, he stuck his hands in the pockets of his well-worn jeans and glared at two of the men, who melted away.

"One for breakfast?" The hostess was not the same one who had been on duty last night.

"I'm with them," he said shortly, nodding toward the laughing group.

David saw him first. "Good morning, Professor Lowell," he called. The third man shrugged and walked away.

Dani swiveled in her chair to watch his approach. Good grief, she thought, and wondered if she'd said the words aloud. Hamp's jeans were well-worn and fit his hard thighs like a dream. The blue-and-white rugby shirt and his running shoes had seen some wear as well. He wore the sleeves pushed up to his elbows and the tail was tucked securely into the jeans, smooth over his flat stomach.

The change was not so much simply in the clothing he wore as in the whole individual. His smile, while retaining a certain amount of reserve, was less formal and more devastating. She supposed that last night, under the coat and tie, he had moved with the grace and agility of an athlete, but the fluid movement of his body hadn't been nearly as conspicuous then as it was now in those tight jeans. She guessed his shoulders had been as broad, his arms as muscular, but their proportion had been camouflaged by fine tailoring.

Dani took a hasty sip of her juice. Or was there a change at all? Was she simply discovering other facets, those other layers, of the man beneath the image? This morning she was in danger of stereotyping him in a totally different way. To her, the look in his eyes, the aura of sensuality he exuded, signified wolf on the prowl.

Sandy patted the chair next to her. "Come and sit down, Daddy. This is Fara and her *pepe*, Pia. Fara has been teaching us some Tahitian."

Hamp acknowledged the introduction and took a seat.

The waiter hurried to pour coffee for him. The young woman uttered a soft goodbye as she moved away.

"*Pepe* means baby," Sandy explained.

David almost choked on his fruit juice and Hamp managed a smile. "I know," he said.

"Oh, of course you do. I keep forgetting that you're an expert." She grinned. "Fara also told Dani and I where the best shopping is in Papeete. I'm dying to buy one of those *pareus*, aren't you, Dani?"

Dani summoned a smile in response to Sandy's enthusiasm. The *pareu* was a colorful sarong type of garment made of soft clingy cotton. She had noticed them on several women and they each seemed to wear them tied in a different way. "If I can learn how to arrange one so it won't fall off."

This time it was Hamp who almost choked. A *pareu* would be even more interesting than his shirt. He remembered bringing one back from a trip several years ago. He couldn't remember who the woman was. Brenda? Or was it Ruth? No matter. He might have forgotten who, but he certainly had a vivid memory of tying, and untying, the garment. "You can buy a book in the hotel gift shop that shows you a number of ways to fasten them," he murmured abstractedly.

Dani lifted her brows. "Oh, really?" she said softly, directing a small, knowing smile toward him.

The smile, of the kind he had speculated about last night, went arrow-straight into his gut, arousing a hot blast of sudden desire stronger than any speculation. Forgotten in an instant were Ruth and Brenda. He felt his heartbeat accelerate, his chest expand and his jeans become uncomfortably snug all in a split second, all with no forewarning, no premonition that might have given him time to prepare himself.

Disoriented by the response, he had to think for a moment to recall his words. Then, understanding that he had made a major slip and hoping his daughter had missed it, he closed his back teeth firmly. A muscle in his jaw reacted, jerking spasmodically as he reached for his coffee cup. He searched in vain for something to say to change the subject.

But Sandy hadn't missed the gaffe. "And how do you know there's a book?" she asked her father. Her expression was suspiciously bland. Then she giggled. "Never mind. I won't ask you to incriminate yourself. I can imagine."

"Sandy," Hamp admonished, while trying to keep a straight face.

"Oh, Daddy, we're all adults here. So you gave a *pareu*, and a book of instructions, to your mistress. So what? I'll bet—"

"Sandy!"

Her father's exclamation shut off any further comment from Sandy, but gazing at him, Dani silently finished the statement for herself. *I'll bet it was fun.* She tried to erase the picture of Hamp laughing huskily as he attempted to arrange the colorful folds of cloth around a naked body.

Her mind had other ideas. Instead of wiping out the image, it elaborated—the *pareu*, slipping precariously, finally abandoned; Hamp's hands and mouth on bare skin, touching, kissing, caressing....

Hamp met Dani's gaze, deliberately holding her prisoner with his dark eyes, as though he could read her thoughts, knew exactly the direction in which her mind was moving. The fact that he was dressed casually in those jeans, which displayed his sex so blatantly, only fueled her imagination.

She was barely aware of her surroundings. Her pulse accelerated, her breathing slowed, she felt a quickening in the lower region of her stomach.

Good Lord! This was just what she'd been determined to avoid. Last night she'd acknowledged his appeal, confident that once she'd faced the problem it would diminish; but her physical reaction this morning was even stronger and more appalling. Wrenching her gaze away, she took a long breath and reached quickly for a grasp on reality as personified by her son. "Have you finished your breakfast, David?" She asked the question she would have asked if he were eight instead of eighteen.

"Yes, Mom," he answered, suspiciously casual.

Oh, mercy. Had the children noticed? "Yes, well—" Damn. She rose, resolution in every line of her body. "I need to get out of this wet suit. Would you like to go into town with me later?"

Before David could reply, Hamp stood, too, sliding his hands into the pockets of his jeans. His manner was different, more determined, when he suggested, "I've chartered a plane to take Sandy and me to Huahine for the day. If David would like to go. . . ."

"Do you mean it, Professor? That would be great!" said David. "Would you mind, Mom?"

"I'd rather go shopping, Daddy," Sandy wailed at the same time.

Both children looked hopefully at their respective parents. Dani was torn. She would have liked to have Sandy's and her son's company, but she hated to deprive David of the opportunity to go with Hamp, a trip that would give him much more pleasure than a day in the city. Then again, if Hamp and David went to Huahine alone, it would defeat their desire for the young people to get to know each other.

Her sensual response of a few moments ago had left her uncharacteristically vague and indecisive. It was all Hamp's fault, she reasoned obscurely. He had deliberately looked at her as if . . . as if he'd . . . like he'd like . . . She abandoned her speculation about his motives and turned to him for a resolution. "What do you think?"

His dark eyes were almost black. His half smile held a trace of anticipation. "It seems we are faced with a dilemma. Do we swap children? Or all stick together? There's plenty of room in the plane. It's up to you." He shrugged, but there was nothing dismissive about the gesture.

His voice was an octave lower. She suspected he was subject to the same arousal she was feeling. Then why had he made the offer? And why had he brought all this up in front of Sandy and David? She swallowed against the dryness in her throat.

"Please, Mom," David urged. "Tomorrow I'll go shopping with you."

Dani turned to her son, smiling at the concession. To David, shopping ranked right up there with having his fingernails pulled out. "You will?"

"Tomorrow we'll all go shopping together," corrected Hamp. "Does that suit you, Sandy?"

"I guess," said Sandy without much enthusiasm.

A trip to Huahine today, shopping tomorrow—the plans seemed to have been finalized without much input from her at all, thought Dani. And what about our resolution not to make this a foursome? The first chance she got, she would put the question to Hamp and he'd better have a damned good answer. At the moment though, his masculine appeal was too hazardous to her well-being, so she avoided that dark gaze completely.

But did she really object? At least the children would be there. Her libido would be forced to behave in their presence. Sure it would—just as it had five minutes ago.

When Dani made no objection, Hamp glanced at his watch. "Fine. Then that's settled," he said, feeling his pulse throb with a high sense of expectancy. Smart or not, the thought of spending two days in the company of this woman was exciting. "Our driver is picking us up at nine. Shall we meet in the lobby?"

"Fine," she echoed. "But I'd like a word alone with you first."

Both David and Sandy were surprised, but they wasted no time making themselves scarce.

When they were alone, Dani turned to Hamp. "I thought we agreed—"

He held up a hand. "I know what you're going to say. But it's just for a couple of days."

She was quiet for a minute. "It isn't simply for the sake of the children, is it, Hamp?"

He smiled, his teeth unbelievably white against the tanned skin of his face. "No, Dani, it isn't for the sake of the children."

"We have nothing in common," she pointed out.

How do you know? thought Hamp, but he decided it was wisest to agree. "Nothing."

"We're very different."

"Very."

"Did you, ah—this is going to sound awfully arrogant— but did you maneuver me into this deliberately?"

"Yeah," he said, drawing a finger down her arm. "I didn't sleep very well last night. Are you mad?"

Dani felt the results of his finger's fiery trail all the way to her toes. "I'll let you know," she said steadily.

FEW PEOPLE KNEW that Dani Fox had any hang-ups at all, but fear of flying was one that she admitted openly. Fortunately she didn't often have to travel by air, and on those occasions when it was unavoidable, she was able to handle her fear in the space and comfort of a large airliner.

When she first saw the small interisland plane she blanched. It was nothing like the silver bullet they had crossed the ocean in. It wasn't even silver but a raw gray color, decorated with regular designs of burnt umber that looked suspiciously like rust. As they drew nearer she noticed that the designs were actually rows of rivets that, she assumed, kept the wings connected to the body of the aircraft.

Her steps slowed. Her head, of its own accord, began to swing from side to side. "No, no, no, no," she chanted softly in time with the movement.

David noticed first. He slung the strap of the camera case over his shoulder and reached for her hand. "Now, Mom," he said gently. "Don't worry. It's perfectly safe."

David never took her fear of flying seriously, thought Dani, as she gripped his fingers in a hold that would have done justice to a sumo wrestler. "How do you know? That is rust there, David. Rust eats away at things like screws and metal. It leaves great big holes."

Sandy, walking ahead of her father, had scrambled up the folding steps and stood by the plane's door, waiting. When Hamp reached the steps, he glanced over his shoulder, then did a double take. Dani was literally as white as her shorts. Shaking her head, she had dug her heels into the tarmac. Every stumbling step was impelled by her son's grasp on her hand. David looked at him helplessly.

Hamp schooled his features to hide a grin of triumph. So there *was* something the independent Mrs. Fox didn't handle with aplomb. The idea pleased him and, oddly, softened his attitude toward her. He didn't have to ask, but he asked anyway, politely, when he'd retraced his steps. "Is something wrong?"

Dani was well past the point of courtesy. "Yes," she blurted. "I'm not too fond of planes in the first place, and I'm certainly not going anywhere in *that* rust bucket. David, let go of my hand."

"Why don't you get on board, David? Here take my duffel bag."

"But . . ."

"Go ahead. I'll talk to your mother."

David dropped her hand. She immediately clenched it into a fist. "It won't do any good to talk," said Dani, her irritation building in response to his take-charge attitude. She knew her fear was irrational, but it was her fear and she'd deal with it as best she knew how—by staying on the ground. "I tell you, Hamp, I'm not going."

She watched David follow Sandy into the bowels of the beast. She blinked. Goodbye, David.

"Dani, I've known the pilot of this plane for years. He's flown me many times before. Do you think I would endanger the life of my daughter, or your son?" Hamp asked gently. "Or you?" he added even more softly.

Her gaze swung to him. "Not deliberately," she conceded. "But accidents happen. David's disappointed in me, but I am not getting on that plane."

Hamp dropped an arm across her shoulders. "I understand how you feel."

"You do?"

"Of course. I'd never insist you go anywhere or do anything you didn't want to do."

"It isn't that I don't want to go, Hamp, but I can't. I just can't walk up those steps."

"The steps," he mused, rubbing his jaw with a forefinger. "Could you walk up them if the plane weren't going to leave the ground?"

"Well, of course," she answered.

He turned her. "Then, come on. Just let David see you're willing to try that much. If I can't make you comfortable enough to fly without fear, I'll let you off."

Her eyes narrowed suspiciously. "You will?"

"I promise." Grinning, he held up two fingers for the Boy Scout pledge.

Grudgingly she turned toward the plane. "Okay, but you'd better keep that promise. I'd probably throw up on you as soon as the wheels left the ground."

His broad hand at her back steadied her as she mounted the steps.

"Mom! Are you going after all?"

Dani didn't miss the enthusiasm in her son's eyes. Hamp answered for her.

"We're trying an experiment," he said as he rambled through Sandy's canvas tote bag. "Sit there, Dani." With a thrust of his elbow he indicated a seat, one of eight on the small plane. "Close the curtain over that window, David. Ah, here we are." He held up a set of earphones connected by a long cord to a tiny tape player. Rambling through the bag again, he came up with a tape. "Do you like the Police?"

Dani nodded. "Yes, do you?" She couldn't hide her surprise.

Hamp grinned. "Sometimes, when I'm in the right mood." He tested the sound, made an adjustment, then hooked the tape player to her belt. "Put these on."

Dani slipped the earphones over her head. "This is very nice of you, but it isn't going to work."

The cord caught in her hair, a strand falling over one brow. Smiling into her eyes, Hamp reached out to smooth it back. His finger hesitated, warm on her cheek, before brushing across her lower lip. The action held them both motionless.

Hamp seemed to shake himself loose more quickly. "You can turn the sound higher, if you like. Now, lean back and relax. Let me . . ." His hand slid under her bottom.

She came to attention, inhaling sharply. "Hamp! What on earth are you doing?" she hissed. Not looking at all repentant, he came up with one end of a seat belt. She snatched it out of his hand. "I'll find the other piece, thank you."

The pilot emerged from the cockpit. "You ready, Perfessor?" he asked, leaning forward to peer with interest over Hamp's shoulder.

"No," said Dani, watching the man with alarm. He was middle-aged, neat, clean—in better condition than his plane, at least.

"Not quite, Jonny. We've got to make the lady very comfortable. She's not too happy about flying in this rust bucket you call a plane."

"Rust bucket!" protested the offended man. He planted his fists on his hips; his eyes narrowed on Dani. "I ain't never had no complaints before."

Ignoring him, Hamp stepped back to examine his handiwork. Dani felt like part of an experiment, hooked up, wired for sound, strapped in. It wasn't a pleasant feeling.

Hamp took the seat beside her, buckled his own seat belt and reached for her hand. He laced his long fingers through hers, warmly and securely. "Do you think you can stand the trip like this?"

Dani took in her surroundings. The pilot was still annoyed, but the cabin was dimly lit—David had pulled all the curtains—so she could ignore his scowl. The music coming through the headphones was pleasant. David smiled his encouragement. Sandy was expectant. And Hamp was holding her hand.

She didn't want to think about how much she was enjoying that. "I guess so. But you'd better keep one of those bags within reach," she said finally, sighing deeply.

3

DANI BREATHED a silent thank-you to the nearest island god for deliverance when the plane's engines finally sighed to a stop. She peeled her fingers away from Hamp's hand, distressed to discover that her nails had left small crescent marks on the back of his hand. "Oh, dear," she murmured, rubbing a finger over them. "Look at your hand. I'm sorry."

"Don't worry about it," Hamp answered enigmatically. "You didn't draw blood." David drew aside his curtain and a stray beam of sunlight reflected off his glasses, masking his expression.

Before she had time to speculate further about the odd huskiness in Hamp's voice, the pilot came out of the cockpit and headed down the narrow aisle.

"Here we are, Perfessor. All safe and sound." The last was delivered with a certain amount of sarcasm and was definitely aimed at Dani.

Dani managed a smile of thanks as the man paused beside their seats. David and Sandy were already unstrapped and on their feet right behind him.

"It was a nice, smooth flight, Jonny," said Hamp.

Jonny nodded, satisfied, and turned away to open the hatch, flooding the compartment with light. He maneuvered the steps into place.

Hamp slung his camera case over his shoulder and stood. Dani reached for her purse.

"I'll be here about five o'clock, Perfessor," said Jonny, as they left the plane.

"Fine. Thanks, Jonny." Hamp waved without turning. "Are you feeling okay?" he asked her.

"I'm fine," she lied. When both feet were firmly on the ground she looked around.

The landing strip on the tiny island of Huahine had been laid parallel to the shore of a peaceful lagoon about thirty yards away. On the beach a wide umbrella in a shade between pink and orange was a single bright accent in the color scheme of azure sky and water, golden sand and lush, verdant vegetation. Sunshine flooded the bucolic landscape as though it had been ladled on.

The runway itself was like something out of a World War II movie, grass dotted and bumpy and hot—very hot. Silence hung in the sweet-smelling air, broken only by the sound of an occasional bird or insect call and the wheezing of the air conditioner that hung precariously from the side of a small concrete building at the edge of the strip.

As the pilot had said, he'd gotten them there. Only marginally able to appreciate the primitive beauty of the scene, Dani groaned silently when she remembered she'd have to face a return trip in a few hours.

Hamp inhaled the clear air and looked around. "Isn't this beautiful? The mountain in the center of the island is Mount Turi," he told her, pointing to a cloud-wreathed peak that looked close enough to touch.

"Yes. It's beautiful," she said flatly.

"Something wrong?"

"I'm already dreading the trip back to Papeete. I hate being treated like some kind of invalid," she muttered more to herself than to him.

Hamp studied Dani's profile for a minute before he commented, "I have an idea that you don't often put yourself into a situation where you might be considered one. It takes a certain amount of bravery to admit a weakness."

The plane's engines came to life behind them. "Are you saying I'm a coward?" Her annoyance was reflected in the quick flare of anger in her green eyes.

He looked away, distracted for a moment by something else. David and Sandy were studiously and rather obviously avoiding each other. Both young faces were closed. During the flight he had been pleased to hear a lively discussion going on between them, though he couldn't make out the words. Clearly it hadn't been a discussion at all but an argument. The careful courtesy with which they had treated each other had been abandoned. He hoped they would work it out. Turning back to Dani, he said, "Not exactly a coward." In an undertone he added, "The kids have had a disagreement."

"They'll get over it. What the hell do you mean, 'Not exactly'?"

Careful to keep his expression bland, he shifted the camera case to his other hand and returned his attention to Dani. "I mean that you don't like to let down your guard, even for a minute."

"I don't know what you're talking about. I certainly let down my guard during that flight. I was holding on to your hand for dear life." Her glorious green eyes dimmed with the admission.

He shrugged. "As you say."

"You are the most exasperating man."

But her fear had been forgotten, thought Hamp, satisfied with his tactic. Pangs of guilt had assaulted him on the plane when her hand had gripped his so tightly. Not until then had he realized just how frightened she really was. He'd wanted her to be with them today, but he wondered if he would have insisted if he'd understood the depths of her fear. Strange, he wouldn't have thought Dani Fox would have been scared of the devil himself.

Several parked vehicles sat in the shade of the concrete building—one, a local version of Le Truck, another, a shiny vintage Trans Am. "There's supposed to be a Jeep waiting for us."

David gave the Trans Am an approving look. "That's a great car," he said.

"It belongs to a friend of mine," Hamp told him.

David grinned, indicating the narrow paved road beyond the building. "Must be exciting to floor the accelerator on a road like that."

"She's probably tried it."

"A woman? This car belongs to a woman?" His grin spread. "Is she married?"

Sandy sniffed at the remark. "I suppose *Smokey and the Bandit* was your favorite movie when you were a little boy," she said, not bothering to hide her disdain.

"One of them. When it was released you probably weren't old enough to appreciate it," he said with his own version of repression.

Sandy made another, more valiant attempt. "Of course, in New York we're exposed to the best in the entertainment field. Most of my friends thought the Bandit movies were rather silly."

"Oh?" countered David as he circled the car, his admiration evident. He gave Sandy a look of mock sympathy. "How sad that your friends in New York had such a narrow outlook. You must love California."

Sandy sniffed, but she didn't try again.

Hiding a smile at the byplay, Dani glanced up to see that Hamp's jaw was clenched in annoyance. She automatically put a hand on his arm. He looked down at her fingers and she made a move to draw back. But he was too quick for her; her fingers were caught in a hard grip. "Come with me," he said heading toward the door of the building. "We'll be back in a minute, kids. Try not to slash each other to ribbons."

"Don't make too much of it, Hamp," she said when they were out of hearing. "It's an emotional age. Besides, David egged her on."

"I can understand why. I'm getting heartily sick of her New York psuedosophistication myself. You'd think California was beyond civilization." He grasped the handle of the glass door and jerked it open with more force than necessary.

"She'll outgrow it," said Dani. "There's an axiom for the parents of teenagers. 'If you don't like the mood they're in, wait five minutes.'"

The air conditioner might have been noisy, but at least it was efficient, she observed, as they stepped out of the bright sunshine into the relative dimness. The room was no more than twelve by twelve and was bisected by a tall counter, waist high on Hamp. It was possibly designed to separate the customers from management, but since it was only six feet long, it was only half effective. A scarred Formica top was littered with maps and pencils, a coffee maker with accoutrements, and some greasy-looking pieces of what Dani supposed were parts of airplane motors.

"Hi, Hamp. Be right with you," came a disembodied but very feminine voice from behind the barrier. Radio static punctuated the words. "Right, Jonny. See you this afternoon. Out."

Hamp leaned one forearm on the counter and looked over to the other side. "Hi, Tenuare. Are you filling in for your brother today?"

"Just for a few minutes. I was doing some snorkeling down at the beach. He had to run into town, but he should be back any minute now with the Jeep." At the same time she spoke, the woman rose. "Hi," she said smiling at Dani. "I'm Tenuare Danton."

Dani was relieved when Hamp finished the introduction, for at the moment she wasn't capable of thought. She considered herself fairly sophisticated, fairly worldly, but the sight that met her eyes robbed her of speech momentarily.

Tenuare Danton was absolutely beautiful. Her skin was the color of wild honey, her features fine drawn and elegant. Her waist-length hair was as black as a moonless night. Startlingly light blue eyes promised all sorts of interesting things. Her body was as gorgeous as the rest of her.

And that lovely body was clothed only in a *pareu*, tied negligently at the hip and bare from the waist up.

Instinctively Dani averted her gaze and began to turn, to give the woman privacy. Her response was automatic and, she thought, natural, one she would have made if she had come upon someone unaware, in an embarrassing state of dishabille. Only at the last moment did she catch herself.

"Tenuare, this is Dani Fox. She and her son are vacationing in Papeete. They came over with us for the day."

Dani smiled, finally finding her voice. "How do you do, Miss Danton?"

"Tenuare, please. How do you do?" she said, and extended her hand across the counter.

Now, Dani, she cautioned herself, as she shook the woman's hand. *You knew from reading about Tahiti that women often go bare like this. They don't think a thing about it, and neither should you. Breasts are just like any other part of the body. Think of them as casually as you would an elbow sticking out there like that.*

The analogy didn't work.

Danielle Fox, the beaches on the Riviera are full of people dressed—or undressed—like this.

I've never been to the Riviera.

It's only because you come from puritanical America that you're startled. Keep a straight face. Don't embarrass your country.

The conversation between Hamp and the beautiful woman was lost to her until Tenuare cocked her head. "I think I hear Travis now. Come on. I'll walk out with you."

David! Good grief.

The radio behind the counter began to squawk. "Oh, dear. You go on." Tenuare waved them out. "I'll catch up with you all later for lunch at the hotel."

Later at the hotel. It seemed she had missed something vital. Well, maybe she would have time for a talk with David, she thought as she followed Hamp back out into the sunlight. Not a lecture, just a quiet word of preparation, though she had no idea what she was going to say. A small frown wrinkled her brow.

She was afraid that 'Don't embarrass your country' wouldn't be quite sufficient to counteract the perfectly normal sexual urges of a teenage boy. Perhaps if Tenuare had been just another woman, less beautifully endowed, she wouldn't have thought anything about it. With a wry smile she remembered her struggle to keep the channels of communication open when David entered puberty. If she could cope with those days she could cope with anything.

Dani gave up trying to devise a plan that wouldn't make an issue of the situation as Hamp introduced her to the handsome young man who had arrived in the dusty Jeep. Travis Danton was as reserved as his sister was open and outgoing. A minimum number of words were exchanged as he handed Hamp the keys and helped Dani into the front seat.

Sandy, who had already climbed into the back with David, seemed to know him, offering a casual, "Hi, Travis."

Strange, Dani had thought this was Sandy's first visit to the islands. As Hamp maneuvered the vehicle onto the narrow road, she asked about the pair.

"Travis and Tenuare are students of mine," he explained. "Their parents are divorced. They live in San Francisco for nine months of the year with their father and spend their summers here on the island with their mother." He chuckled softly. "I think they would prefer paradise year-round, but their father insisted on an American education."

That explained how Sandy had known the young man. Dani digested the information, wondering at the contrast of cultures the two youngsters experienced by such a swap. She was slightly ashamed of her reaction to Tenuare's partial nudity. "They seem young," she observed.

"They just had their twenty-first birthday. Twins, as a matter of fact."

Her curiosity satisfied, Dani sat back in her seat and concentrated on the scenery. Hamp gave them a running commentary as he drove, pointing out the vanilla fields they passed, explaining that the vanilla plants had to be cross-pollinated by hand.

Lush greenery lined the sides of the road, often growing together over their heads to form a vivid canopy. They passed a small farm where a woman was filling a large basket with ripe shiny melons. On another a man hoed a potato vine. Children played in neatly swept yards, their golden bodies round with health, their high-pitched giggles like music when they waved at the passing vehicle.

Dani enjoyed Hamp's commentary as much as she did the scenery—delivered as it was in his deep voice. She could imagine him in a classroom, weaving tales to enthrall his students.

She sighed in contentment. "This is more like what I always expected Tahiti to be."

He smiled. "Don't let anyone hear you call this Tahiti. Tahiti is only the name of the island where you landed. The group is called the Society Islands."

"I knew that," she said. "But everyone refers to it as Tahiti."

"Not everyone. These islands were once separate kingdoms. And there still remains a residual feeling of independence, especially among some of the elders who look on the growth in Papeete as the downfall of island culture. Most of their children leave home early—there are no high schools on Huahine. They go to Mooréa or Papeete to finish school and stay to find employment, or simply more excitement. When they return, if they return at all, their values have usually changed drastically."

"Like the twins'?" asked Dani.

The idea made her sad until Hamp explained, "No, the twins have done just the opposite. Though their father would like for them to remain in the United States, they cling to the island culture their mother has instilled in them. They plan to come back here after graduation."

They passed through quaint villages with musical names: Haapu, Parea, Maroe. Before long, Hamp turned off the main road that circled the island to park at the edge of a lake. To their right was a square patch of ground about fifty by thirty meters, delineated by a low rock wall. He switched off the motor and the silence was immediate and complete.

"A *marae*. Is this Manus?" David spoke with wonder, the first time since they'd left the airport, a hush in his voice to match the hush of the place.

Hamp smiled at David's response. "The best known of the ancient temples," he clarified for Dani. "Of the twenty-eight that have been discovered along this lakeside, sixteen have been restored." A hand on the frame of the windshield, he swung his long legs to the side and jumped out in a smooth, well-coordinated maneuver. "Come on, I'll give you the tour."

David took it all in, fascinated. Even Sandy was quiet.

"That's the *ahu*, or altar, up there," Hamp said. He pointed toward the water. Along its edge a platform of volcanic rock three steps up from ground level had been built in the shape of a pyramid.

Dani was moved by the beauty and stillness of the place. "No walls in their places of worship to separate them from nature's grace." She spoke in a low tone.

"None," said Hamp, shooting her a long look, then turning back to the scene. "During the ceremonies everyone sat on the ground facing the altar." He indicated slabs of upright granite, which because of their shape and size, Dani had taken for tombstones. "These are the backrests for the royal members of nearby tribes. On feast days the services could drag on for a long time and they got tired. The smaller stones were for the lesser leaders."

"What's that?" asked Sandy, pointing to a huge thatched building built on stilts out over the placid water.

"That's a reproduction of the council hall. It's surprisingly authentic. Go on over and have a look if you want to. On boat days the local people set up booths to sell carved-shell jewelry and hand-dyed *pareus*. Today isn't boat day or Le Truck wouldn't have been parked at the airport. But there might be someone working in there."

"Boat day? As in cruise ships?" asked Dani. "I can't believe they'd let great hordes of tourists tramp over this lovely place."

"They don't tramp around much. Huahine is somewhat off the beaten track—for now."

Sandy wandered off. David directed a question to Hamp, something about migrations.

"Hawaii was settled by some of the islanders from here, a bold group who couldn't live under the conditions that existed at that time. They wanted to escape the constant warring that went on between the island kingdoms so they stocked their canoes and, heading north, set off on a vast empty sea for a land they only knew of in ancient legends."

He looked beyond the altar, focusing on an inner image. "Tribes of people had migrated over the centuries all the way from the Malay peninsula. Generations before them had island-hopped across the Pacific from Australia to New Zealand, from Fiji to Samoa to here, so there were precedents, however vague and lost in history they were. The old stories, handed down from father to son, from mother to daughter, filled them with hope of finding another place. But these people knew less about navigation than Columbus did and they didn't even have the North Star to guide them when they set out, not until they reached the Northern Hemisphere."

The emotion in his voice touched Dani. "I have an idea that if you'd lived here then, you'd have led the way," she said after a long pause.

He did look at her then and smiled, a bit embarrassed at his own passion. "You're probably right. I guess I'm a frustrated explorer. Sorry if I sounded like a professor."

"Oh, no, sir. That is, you do, but we don't mind, do we, Mom?" David protested; he'd hung on to every word.

"Not at all," said Dani.

But it was clear that Hamp was finished for now. David, too, wandered off.

Hamp watched him go. "It's exciting when you find a student with significant ability, like David."

Yes, thought Dani. Teaching would fill some of the needs of an explorer. As a modern-day man he had chosen to find his excitement in sharing his knowledge, in nurturing other scholars. But, whimsically, she could also imagine Hamp—even after knowing him such a short time and especially after witnessing the variations in his personality—at the helm of a ship or striding forth over unknown territory in search of some profound, ultimate truth. Or maybe with a knife in his teeth.

Hamp looked at her with a steady gaze. There was so much more to this woman than was apparent on the surface. He was discovering another, more interesting layer each time he was with her. "I should have realized that he didn't come by it alone."

Dani had to make a conscious effort to impress David's image over the image of Hamp in seventeenth century garb. "I don't understand," she said.

He raked an impatient hand through his sun-streaked hair. "I did realize it—last night when I called you an extraordinary woman." He shoved both hands into his pockets, staring fixedly at her. "A lot of people come here with the idea that the early inhabitants were primitive savages, just as a lot of people have the same conception of the American Indian. I should have known that you would see beneath that."

Dani was oddly embarrassed by the praise and strangely moved by the warmth in his eyes. It was time to inject something light into the conversation. She checked to be sure her son was out of earshot, relieved to be free of both children's presence for a minute. As the youngsters disappeared inside the thatch-roofed building, she turned to him with a half smile. "Speaking of David, I offered you the benefit of my great experience with teenagers, now may I ask your advice about something?"

"Of course."

"How do you think I should approach David about the island custom of going topless."

He smiled. "I wondered if that had bothered you."

"I wasn't bothered." She grinned, relenting honestly. "Well, maybe a little surprised at first. I mean, it isn't an everyday occurrence in Palo Alto to see a beautiful woman minus her top. But I was wondering about David's reaction. Teenage boys' libidos are sometimes rather fragile, Hamp. I want him to be prepared."

"I think David can handle it." He winced at his own double entendre. "Sorry."

"I should hope so," she said, not hiding her amusement. "But seriously, Hamp, don't you think I should have a talk with him?"

"Dani, David will be fine. He's more mature than you give him credit for being. It might take him a few minutes to adapt, but the adjustment will come quicker if you don't make an issue of it—"

"I don't intend to make an issue of anything," she objected. "And I thought you were the one who didn't know much about teenagers."

"Then why did you ask me?"

"I had the notion that, as a male, you might have something of value to contribute."

"I do know something about boys and their reaction to lovely women," he grinned wryly. "David will be surprised, just as you were, at first. He may even goggle a bit. But after a few minutes he'll begin to accept her nudity as the reality of another culture. It's all in the psychological conception of what you see. If my great-grandfather had gotten a glimpse of my great-grandmother's ankle he would have been turned on. I barely noticed Tenuare's breasts because I've been here so often. In the islands it's not unusual to see women without their tops. I've grown accustomed to it." He hesitated. "No, I take that back."

I thought so, said Dani to herself. You'd have to be blind not to.

"Let me see if I can explain. I do notice them, but it's just the same as my noticing that Tenuare has beautiful legs."

Dani didn't believe that for a minute. No man could have ignored . . .

Still, she decided she would take his advice. She wouldn't mention anything to David. He was right; David was mature beyond his years. She often had a tendency to try to coddle her uncoddleable son.

"Okay, I won't say anything."

"I think that's wise."

"I suppose you're right. When in Rome, and so forth. If I took my top off it wouldn't mean a thing." Oh, Lord. Why on earth had she said that?

He held her with his dark, coffee-brown eyes; time seemed to be a long, drawn-out thread between them, a thread that threatened to snap if Dani dared to breathe. Finally he spoke, but if she had hoped for some casual comment to relieve the tension caused by her careless remark, she was sadly disappointed.

"Try me," he challenged half seriously, reaching for her hand. His thumb slid over the pulse point on the inside of her wrist. "My psychological perception of you is entirely different, Dani. Not that you don't have gorgeous . . . legs. I look forward to seeing more of them."

His voice was low as his eyes scanned her, lingering longest on the body part in question. Her neat white shorts and matching tailored safari shirt might as well have been made of cellophane. She felt her pulse skip in response; he couldn't have missed it.

"No," he went on. "On second thought, I'll have to settle for a kiss right now. Our kids might get an education far more advanced than what they're ready for."

"This isn't the time or place for this sort of thing, Hamp," she said, sorry her voice sounded so wishy-washy. "Let me go."

He looked around. "I think it's a perfect place. Beautiful, peaceful, quiet—" his lips curved "—deserted, at the moment."

Dani's legs were weak. Her pulse was like thunder in her ears. So when he hooked an arm around her waist and slowly drew her closer, there was not resolution enough in her to sustain her objection. His broad palm slid from her waist to the small of her back, urging her body to adjust, fitting her soft curves to his hard planes. Each one of his long fingers left a warm, exciting impression on her skin. It was as though her clothing were a conductor of heat and electricity.

"No, Hamp." She wiggled uncomfortably, felt his burgeoning reaction to her movement and was still. "Look, I have no objections to one kiss, but this is a place of worship. I'd feel as if I was kissing in church or something."

Smiling, Hamp looked down at her moist lips and knew his hunger could never be appeased by one kiss. He felt all the blood in his body heat as it rushed to nourish the heaviness in his loins. He raised a brow, his smile grew into a grin, but he didn't release her. Instead he tightened his arm around her waist and lifted her until her toes dangled several inches off the ground.

"What are you—" Her hands moved up to his shoulders to brace herself. He admired the strength of her fingers. This was no fragile, delicate female, despite her small size.

Taking several long strides to reach the far side of the *marae*, he stepped over the low wall. Only when they were hidden under the fragrant boughs of a huge mango tree, did he let her slide down his body until she stood between the slight spread of his legs. Lord, she felt good there. His gaze dropped to her mouth. Her lips were faintly moist and tempting—so tempting.

"Hamp, I don't think—" And that was the truest thing Dani had said all day. She didn't think. The minute his head dipped, the minute his firm lips touched hers, all rational thought was an impossibility. It was a gentle but determined assault, an invasion she realized she'd been waiting for, wanting, from the first words they'd exchanged. She'd lied to herself when she pretended otherwise.

Her arms moved of their own accord across his broad shoulders to wind around his neck, her fingertips seeking the sun-warmed texture of his hair. He moaned softly, the sound escaping from deep in his throat, then changed the angle of the kiss. His tongue, moist and hungry, explored her mouth, met her own, tasting, teasing, searching.

A voice faintly pierced the haze that seemed to surround them. "Daddy. Dani. Come see what we've found."

Hamp slowly, reluctantly, broke off the kiss. He raised his head, shaking it once to clear his thoughts. He looked down at the woman in his arms, her eyes slightly glazed, her lips slightly swollen, and felt an unnamed emotion that he'd never felt before. She withdrew her arms from around his neck, letting her hands rest lightly on his chest. She couldn't possibly miss the pounding under her fingers. He released her and took a step back, as though from a fire that had grown too hot. "Are you okay?" he asked quietly.

His daughter's voice reached them again. "I wonder where they are."

"I'm fine," Dani answered him.

Hamp sighed and moved away from the tree. "We'll be right there, honey," he called.

Silently they traversed the path to the council house. Dani was aware of Hamp's eyes boring into her back. She won-

dered what she would see if she turned to him. The kiss had
shaken her deeply; was he equally disturbed by its effects?

Had she turned she would have seen Hamp's inner tur-
moil reflected in his eyes. As he followed her down the path,
he tried to ignore the sensual sway of her hips, the fevered
touch of the sunlight on her hair. The kids were waiting, he
warned himself. But it took a tremendous effort for him to
force down his desire and guard his expression from both
Dani and his daughter.

David and Sandy met them at the entrance to the council
house, which was one large room, with half walls and a
thatched roof similar to the dining room at the hotel. David looked bored, which surprised Dani. Her son wasn't
often bored.

Sandy, however, was bubbling over. She had discovered
one of the island women arranging a display of hand-dyed
pareus. The colors were rich and profuse and the hems
traced with intricate designs—fish and shells, palms,
flowers, sails. Each length of fabric was different and each
resembled a delicate watercolor painting. "Aren't they
beautiful, Dani? Daddy, may I have one? Please?"

"Which do you like?" asked her father.

Sandy held up a sunny yellow *pareu*, its hem defined by
stylized palm trees in bronze. "You have to get one, too,
Dani. We can wear them to dinner tonight." In fluent
French, Hamp began a bargaining process with the woman
at the table.

Dani wandered to a clothesline that had been strung di-
agonally across a corner of the huge room. A breeze stirred
several of the *pareus*, stretched over the cord to show the
designs to their best advantage. She was lured to a length
of fabric dyed a soft shade of lilac. The hem featured lush
hibiscus blossoms in a darker shade of the same color with

soft, jade leaves. She fingered the material, then dropped it suddenly when she noticed that her hand was trembling.

"I like that one, Mom," said David quietly from behind her.

Hoping that her son hadn't noticed her shaking hand, she smiled over her shoulder. "The men wear them, too, you know. Maybe I should buy it for you."

"Nah, Mom." He grinned. "Lilac isn't my color." Making the decision for her, he reached up to remove the garment from the cord. "But you'd look good in it. And you'd appreciate the work that went into making it. Unlike our friend over there, who just wants something new to wear," he added sarcastically.

Uh-oh. She forced lightness into her voice. "Every woman likes new clothes. And it is a beautiful thing. Okay, I think I'll indulge myself." She hoped Hamp had been right about the book of instructions; if not, she could always wear it as a beach cover-up.

"Good. Too bad it isn't from Noo Yor-rk." He rolled his eyes as he emphasized the words.

She took the fabric from his hands and began to fold it, giving herself a chance to think. "David, it isn't like you to be irritable or brusque. I don't like it."

"I'm sorry," he responded stiffly. "I didn't realize I would offend you."

"Good grief, now you sound like the professor. Don't get all horsey with me. I am still the mother here, you know. And we are still the guests of the Lowells for the day. I expect you to be polite and cheerful."

He deflated. "Yeah. Okay."

She led the way to the small table where the woman waited with her cash box. Dani's high-school French was almost nonexistent but she gave it a try, aware that Hamp was listening with amusement to her bargaining efforts.

When they'd finished their business, Hamp clapped his hands, rubbing them together in an attempt at heartiness. "Anybody hungry?" he asked.

David and Sandy answered enthusiastically and Dani wondered if Hamp and Sandy had had the same talk she and David had had. She nodded, too. "I'm starving."

They collected their packages and returned to the Jeep.

The Hotel Bali Hai was more like what she'd envisioned a hotel in Tahiti to be, she thought, as Hamp parked the car. Thatch-roofed, the main building was positioned at the edge of a blue lagoon. Some of the tiny cottages sat on stilts over the water, other slightly larger ones with more than one room were half hidden along flower-strewn walkways. But nowhere did one get the impression of a large, self-contained hotel.

As they approached the entrance to the dining room Dani saw Sandy and David talking to Tenuare. The young woman's *pareu*, Dani noted with a smile, was now knotted as a sarong instead of as a skirt.

Hamp dropped an arm over Dani's shoulder and bent until his mouth was close to her ear. "Tenuare was at the beach this morning," he explained in a low voice. "She came inside to monitor the radio for her brother. But she wouldn't go topless in a public restaurant."

The warmth of his breath distracted her enough to cause her to relax slightly in his casual embrace. "I'm not familiar with the island etiquette," she said, "but I'd already decided to take your advice and trust David's maturity."

"Wise decision." His fingers on her shoulder tightened in affectionate response.

Unbidden her eyes flew up to clash with his.

"Wise woman," he added, brushing her lips lightly with his.

Dani forced her gaze to the front to find all three of the people waiting for them wearing odd expressions. David's was stunned, Sandy's, wary, and Tenuare's, speculative.

4

THE TRIP BACK to Papeete was comparatively uneventful. Dani, who had been so frightened on the way out, was quietly reflective and almost calm. She had seen so much, experienced so many conflicting emotions over the past hours, that she had plenty to take her mind off the ordeal of flying. The memory of Hamp's kiss, not to mention the altercation between David and Sandy, was more than enough to distract her from the forty minutes of the flight.

A light, almost misty rain was falling over the island of Tahiti when the plane landed at Faaa. But the late-afternoon sun reappeared just as they left the terminal. Dani inhaled the freshly washed air appreciatively and sighed. They approached the waiting limousine. She met David's rueful smile as the chauffeur doffed his cap and opened the door for her.

Hamp didn't miss the exchange. "What's funny?" he asked, looking to David for the explanation.

"I promised Mom a ride in one of these when I get rich."

"And I told him that limousines weren't my style. Too fancy. I prefer Le Truck."

"Tomorrow we'll take Le Truck when we go into town to shop."

David groaned. "I'd forgotten about that."

Dani's laughter was like a summer rain, thought Hamp, light and cool and refreshing. He couldn't resist returning her smile.

Sandy smiled, too. "I hadn't forgotten. Had you, Dani?"

"Not on your life."

The foursome separated at the entrance to the hotel after deciding to meet an hour later for dinner. Dani agreed to the arrangement with only a small thought for the plans she and Hamp had made only last night to go their own way. Those plans were gone—if not with the wind, then on a soft Pacific breeze.

After the altercation at the airport, David and Sandy had reached a point where they were at least tolerant of each other. Lunch had been a pleasant experience; afterward Hamp and David had gone back to the site while she, Tenuare and Sandy had slathered themselves with sunscreen and laid out to bake. She and Sandy had kept their tops on.

She hurried to her room. A long, cool shower refreshed her, but then she had to decide what to wear. She had promised Sandy that she would try on the *pareu*, but even after Tenuare had given them a demonstration of tying it, even realizing that it was a much more versatile garment than she had imagined, she still thought it more suited to be worn as a beach cover-up. Clad only in bikini panties, she stood in front of the open closet and contemplated her travel wardrobe with a frown.

At home she had no such problems. She shopped carefully, having neither the time nor the money for mistakes. Her weight never varied more than a pound or two, so everything always fit. She liked bright colors and most of them complemented her coloring. So, at home, she simply reached into her closet for the first thing that was clean. She now did the same thing, annoyed with herself for vacillating. Coming up with an emerald-green shirtwaist, she put it back. The *pareu* lay across her bed, its lovely lilac color a much more tempting sight.

With the fabric in her hands, she stood before the full-length mirror on the back of the closet door. Keeping the design at the bottom, she stretched the length of fabric across her back and brought it around as Tenuare had shown her. She crossed the two ends in front and gathered the excess material, twisting the ends a couple of times. Then she brought them up to tie at the back of her neck.

Suddenly the flat length of material became a beautifully shaped dress. The folds draped slightly from the center twist to camouflage the fact that she was not wearing a bra. She'd wondered about that. She turned. The fabric dipped a bit in back gracefully, and softly hugged her hips.

She stepped back from the mirror and gasped aloud at her first overall view of herself. The image that stared back at her was one of clear and open invitation.

Barefoot, with her wild hair spilling across her shoulders and with her face scrubbed clean, a trace of lip color her only remaining makeup, she looked like a primitive maiden ready for some bizarre mating ritual. Or the luminary in a red-light district. Even onstage dressed in one of her sequined gowns, wearing what David called her ski makeup—an inch of powder on an inch of base—she had never looked so—loose was the only word that came to mind.

"Uh-uh," she said out loud to the woman in the mirror. "This will not do." She'd fought this image all her adult life, realizing from an early age that her appearance, her thick red hair and her rounded curves, were rather provocative without any help from audacious clothes. She liked to look good. What woman didn't? She liked bright colors and unusual jewelry, but she was always careful to maintain a certain caution in the way she dressed.

She reached up to untie the *pareu*, intending to remove the outrageous garment when her hands were stilled by a knock on the door.

David. She hurried to the door, speaking before she had it all the way open. "Honey, you'll have to give me a minute more. I'm not . . ." The words trailed off.

Hamp's jaw was slack. He stared at her, dumbfounded. "You look . . ." His words trailed off, too. He used the hand that held a flower to gesture.

"I know what I look like," she informed him with asperity. His stare, like that of a hungry panther, was easy to read. She kept her hand on the edge of the door. "I was just going to change. Where are David and Sandy?"

Hamp vaguely heard Dani asking him a question. It wasn't like him to be thrown this way. Not even this morning when they'd kissed in the *marae*, had he felt this disoriented. It was imperative that he regain his balance, and quickly. What was her question? Oh, yes, the kids. "Upstairs," he murmured. "Don't change."

"Hamp, I have to. I can't go to dinner looking like this."

She had begun to move the door toward him, to shut him out, and the notion was suddenly unbearable. Stop it, he cautioned himself. She's just another woman. But reflexively he put out a hand to stop the motion of the door. His mind clicked on all cylinders, seeking a solution. "You're fine," he said. Never had the word been used in such a milksop way, he realized in disgust. He tried again. "Sandy's wearing her *pareu*, too. You'll disappoint her if you change."

She turned back to survey herself once more in the mirror and he got his first view of her backside, the soft material clinging to her sweet fanny like a lover's caress. He made a noise that sounded, even to his own ears, like a predator on the prowl.

Dani shot him a look that spoke volumes and shook her head. "No, it's too much."

Suddenly, disregarding the danger to his libido, he stepped inside the room, took the door from her hand and closed it behind him.

"Hey, wait just a minute. . . ."

He ignored her protest. "Nonsense," he said, glad that his voice had reverted to its normal tone. "You're overreacting. When you get your shoes on and, uh, your hair arranged, you'll be fine."

Dani searched his face for deception, then looked once more at her reflection. She was uncertain. "Are you sure? I wouldn't want to embarrass David."

"I'm sure," Hamp guaranteed her. She looked beautiful. She wasn't going embarrass anyone, but she sure as hell was going to strain his control to the limit. He anticipated the struggle with relish.

"All right. I'll give it a try." When Hamp made no move to leave, Dani said, "Why don't I meet you in the dining room? It won't take me long to finish dressing."

She still didn't sound convinced. "Why don't I wait for you here?" he suggested. He knew as well as he knew his name that if he walked out of here she'd change.

As Dani watched, he settled himself against the headboard of her bed as though he belonged there. He yanked a pillow from under the spread and slid it behind his back. When he was comfortably arranged, he spun the flower in his hand by its stem. "Hurry up, we'll miss the sunset."

The familiarity and intimacy of the pose annoyed Dani. "Hamp, I'd like you to leave."

"Why? You're decently covered. The kids are in the lobby listening to a lecture on scuba diving."

Her irritation was quick to surface and was mirrored in the sudden flare of her green eyes. She searched his features, but could find no hint of the guile she knew was there. His eyes were inscrutable behind his glasses. She'd like to see him without them, would like to discover if his thoughts would be more easily read if he didn't have the glasses on. Realizing another protest would seem childish, she silently hid her simmering anger beneath a calm facade and went about arranging her unruly hair, twisting, pinning, until the mass was finally subdued.

Hamp watched Dani's movements with a growing feeling of wonder. She was obviously irked by him, yet her movements were not the jerky ones of anger. She was the most graceful thing he'd ever seen—like a butterfly, he thought whimsically, the way her hands fluttered over her hair, pinning, tucking. He noticed for the first time that her hands were lovely. The nails were buffed and not too long. Her arms were slender, her shoulders smooth and rounded and exquisite. Funny. He'd not noticed, either, how very feminine she was.

She turned, her body in half profile to him, and he felt the air leave his lungs. When she raised her arms the motion lifted her breasts, too, and he realized all at once that she wasn't wearing a bra. He came up off the bed with a surge of energy. Plunging one hand into the pocket of his slacks he walked to the sliding door overlooking the pool.

Dani eyed his back as she reached under the dresser for the shoes she'd worn last night. He stood with his weight on one hip, his forearm on the frame of the sliding door. Absently he raised the flower he was still holding to his nose. She remembered one of her first impressions of him: that he was as stable as a rock. She knew from being held against his body that the man who stood looking out her door was rock hard and all male, but susceptible enough to enjoy the scent of a simple flower.

A strange sort of panic gripped her, suddenly and without warning. She fought it by taking a deep breath and letting it out slowly. With a hand on the edge of the furniture she slipped one of her shoes on and then the other. Straightening, she felt better. The added height bolstered her confidence and with the addition of civilized accoutrements the *pareu* became just another sundress. She slicked on a bit more lip gloss and picked up her purse. "I'm ready."

Hamp turned. "There. You look terrific," he said with a smile. "Didn't I tell you?"

"I hate people who are always right."

"Not always," he said, but more to himself than to her. "Here, this is for you. Women here in Tahiti usually wear flowers in their hair in the evening." He held out the single blossom. "*Tiare* is to Tahiti what the lotus is to India."

Dani took the blossom. "And what is that?" she asked. The scent of the creamy white flower was vaguely gardenialike but more discreet. Its velvet petals caressed her cheek as she anchored it behind her left ear.

"Symbolic. A charm. It's the only flowering plant that was here before the Polynesians arrived. So, to them, it has a special magic."

"Thank you," she said coolly, not yet ready to forget her irritation at the way he'd bulldozed his way into her room.

He was standing close, too close. He lifted a finger to touch the petal of the flower with an absent sort of smile that she hadn't seen before and didn't trust for a second. Then he traced the curve of her ear with the same finger.

"Hamp, we seem to have lost sight of our original goals."

"You mean the kids?"

She shook her head slightly against the pressure of the finger as though to brush away an annoying insect. "Yes. Today has been pleasant. I've enjoyed it. . . ."

His finger had reached her jaw. "But you can't forget that kiss." He smiled, a slow, sexy half smile. "Neither can I."

His smile, along with the effect of that roving finger and her earlier panicked feeling, fueled her anger. "I mean it,

Professor." She bit the words out, leaving no doubt that every one of them was significant, as she firmly grasped his wrist. "I was under the impression that we had reached some kind of understanding. I hope I wasn't mistaken," she added pointedly.

That was before he'd seen the wild beauty in the *pareu*, Hamp thought. These few minutes in her room had changed everything as far as he was concerned. He held against her grip for an endless minute as their eyes did battle. Finally he relented; there would be another time. He dropped his hand to his side. "Shall we go to dinner?" he asked easily.

Dani was tempted to pursue the subject, but she decided to let sleeping professors lie.

THE MAN at the microphone was good at his job, observed Dani, as they watched the last of the dinner show provided by the hotel. He had the guests introducing themselves, telling where they were from, extolling the praises of the islands.

Dani joined in the general laughter. She touched her ear, setting in motion one of the small earrings that were a gift from Sandy. Mother-of-pearl, carved in the shape of tiny *ti'i*, the islands' equivalent of totems, they dangled exquisitely on a thin gold wire. Sandy, who was sitting to her right, caught the movement and smiled.

"I love them," whispered Dani.

"I'm glad," Sandy whispered back. "I couldn't remember if you had pierced ears. The gift shop has some really great stuff, but Daddy said we should wait to see what Papeete has before we buy a lot."

Dani nodded sagely, trying to hide a smile. "That's probably a good idea." Sandy was, as she'd first noticed in the airport waiting area, one of the mall generation. Dani felt a pang at the thought of her growing into womanhood without the guidance of a mother. Hamp was trying, but Sandy was obviously an enigma to him at times. Still, she had managed fairly well with the *pareu* having tied it over one shoulder in the manner of a Roman toga. It was quite effective and made her look older than her years. Rather, it made her look like a young girl trying to look older than her years.

The master of ceremonies had finished at the table next to them. He held the microphone toward Sandy. "And what is your name, *madame*?" he joked.

Sandy giggled. "Sandy Lowell. I'm from—California," she answered, only stumbling slightly over the last word. She hesitated for a moment, glancing at Dani, then announced to the entire place that they had a famous singer in their midst—Danielle Fox of San Francisco.

Dani aimed a kick in the direction of Sandy's foot and missed. "I'm not even *from* San Francisco," she hissed.

"Who here ever heard of Palo Alto?" Sandy whispered back with a grin.

Dani would have liked to sink under the table. Unfortunately that was impossible.

"Will you sing a number for us?" asked the master of ceremonies. The audience erupted with encouragement.

Dani's eyes went around the table. David clapped politely, but his face was a mask. Hamp smiled with only slightly more warmth. No help there.

There was nothing to do but acquiesce gracefully. "I'll get you for this," she promised Sandy in an undertone as she rose and accepted the microphone.

"Do you know 'The Hawaiian Wedding Song'?" she asked the bandleader. The haunting melody was one of her favorites.

The man nodded and raised his hand.

After the first few notes, sung in Dani's clear mezzo-soprano, the emcee signaled to someone behind him. It was clear that he'd expected a novice, but quickly recognized a professional. At his signal the lights dimmed and the spotlight came on again, fixing Dani in its mellow glow. The audience stilled; even the waiters paused in their serving of after-dinner drinks.

"'I can feel my heart singing. . . .'"

Hamp sat transfixed. He could no more have torn his gaze from the woman who sang like an angel than he could have halted his heartbeat by willpower alone. She was breathtaking. And he was being drawn deeper and deeper under her spell, hypnotized by her beauty, her spirit, her grace.

"'Blue skies of Hawaii smile, on this, our wedding day.'"

He held his breath, waiting.

"'I do, love you, with all my heart.'"

As the last note faded away, the spotlight slowly narrowed to a pinpoint and disappeared completely, plunging the room into darkness. The audience paid her the ultimate compliment—silence—for a full thirty seconds. Then the applause began.

Hamp joined in, but his applause was automatic, his face expressionless. The words of the coda—the simple and beautiful vow that ended the song—affected him as he'd never been affected before. What the hell was happening to him?

To be honest, something had already happened. The question should be, how deeply was he going to allow himself to be involved? He watched Dani make her way back to the table and rose as she approached. The music of the Hawaiian ballad had obviously moved her, too, leaving her eyes misty.

The emcee might have asked for an encore, but the expression in Hamp's eyes stopped him. Instead, over the sound of the applause, he said, "I hope you plan to be at Maeva Beach for a few days. We'd like to hear you again."

Dani moved her shoulders noncommittally, trying to shake off the effects of the song.

"That was absolutely beautiful, Dani," said Sandy, subdued for once.

"Great, Mom," said David carefully.

"Thank you, honey." She managed a smile for her son, then turned to the young girl. "Sandy, if you ever do anything like that to me again, I'll wring your neck. I'm on vacation, remember?"

"I promise I won't," said Sandy. Then her elfin face was transformed by a grin. "But it was worth it."

Hamp cleared his throat. "I suppose life in the spotlight can be perturbing."

David's reaction was instant and furious. "Don't say that!" he declared with angry spirit. "You have no idea how hard my mother works. Life for her is no picnic, believe me—spotlight or not. She—"

Stunned by his outburst, Dani laid a hand on his arm. "David," she said, interrupting quietly. She was surprised at the tension she felt under her fingers. "I don't think Hamp intended to be insulting. But you're very close yourself." She tempered her criticism with a smile of love. "Thanks, honey, but I don't need a champion."

He slumped, his backbone rounding in frustration, his chin sinking to his chest. "I'm sorry, Mom. I know you don't. Sorry, Professor Lowell."

Hamp touched the boy's shoulder. "I understand, David. I would have been disappointed if you hadn't defended your mother. Although she's right. Truly, I didn't mean my remark to be offensive."

"I understand, too, Professor, and I do apologize."

Hamp had an idea that mother and son needed a few minutes of privacy. But he sure as hell wasn't ready to turn in for the night, not until he had learned the outcome of this situation—and danced with Dani. He looked around. The band had begun to play. Couples were moving onto the floor. "I think it's about time you make sure your mother fully understands the reasons for your anger," he suggested to David.

David's eyes met his in understanding. The boy nodded and Hamp turned to his daughter. "Sandy, I think we'd better dance."

Sandy, who had been listening to the exchange with avid interest, said, "Why?"

"Sandy." His tone held an unmistakable note of command.

She sighed and put her hand into her father's outstretched one. "Okay," she answered reluctantly.

When they were alone, Dani asked her son, "What did Hamp mean about your anger? Have I missed something, David?"

David's gaze was fixed miserably on his hands. "It's just that I get so mad—I hate to see you have to work so hard. If I were out of school, I could have a full-time job...."

"David, look at me. I want to ask you a question and I want a straight answer."

"Sure."

He seemed perplexed by the no-nonsense demand, and well he might be, thought Dani. As far as she knew, her son had never lied to her. "Does it embarrass you that I have a nightclub, that I sing in one?"

His surprise was instant and genuine. She settled back in her chair, awaiting his answer, knowing what it would be before he spoke. She cursed herself for jumping to conclusions.

"Of course it doesn't embarrass me. I'm proud of you. You have a terrific voice. Maybe you could be on TV if you didn't have to—"

"Stop right there." She leaned forward to grasp one of his hands in both of hers. She was sure her smile could have lit the room. "Oh, honey, I have an idea we have been misunderstanding each other's motives for a long while. From now on, I want to make mine perfectly clear. I have absolutely no interest in expanding my career. I'm doing exactly what I want to be doing. I won't say we have no money problems, but they're manageable now. I wouldn't let you support me if you could. But it's not just you. I wouldn't let anyone support me. I've grown too independent for that."

David digested all this for a minute. "And you thought I was embarrassed because you own a nightclub?" he asked. "Mom, how could you think such a thing?" He seemed more relaxed and relieved than she had seen him in weeks. "I'm very proud of you."

"I'm sorry for misunderstanding, honey. We should have discussed it before now." She squeezed the hand she still held. "You want to dance with an old lady?" she asked.

Hamp watched the two move onto the dance floor. They were both smiling. He'd suspected that all they needed was to talk. Not as mother to son, but as friend to friend. A little prod from an objective bystander was all it had taken, he thought, satisfied.

When the music died away he and Sandy were next to Dani and David. "Shall we change partners for the next one?" he suggested as though the idea had just occurred to him.

Dani agreed, and though the teenagers didn't look thrilled, they didn't protest. "That was smooth," said Dani when the next dance began and she was in his arms. Too smooth. She knew she had to thank him for his perception, but for some reason she wasn't looking forward to doing so.

"What?" Hamp drew back to look down at her, a half smile curving his lips. "Oh, you mean getting the kids to dance together." His eyes glittered behind the glasses. "I have to admit that wasn't my motive at all. I wanted to hold you," he drawled evenly. "Among other things."

The warm hand at her back gave her the feeling of being sheltered. She had never liked the feeling before, had fought against it on more than one occasion, in fact. With Hamp it was different. He was offering protection, but wasn't insisting that she accept it. Such an offer was twice as dangerous as an overt proposition, twice as hard to fight. "Perhaps I haven't made my feelings clear."

"You made your feelings perfectly clear," he answered ambiguously. "Relax, Dani. Let's dance." Again he brought her close.

There was nothing provocative about the way he was holding her, nothing you wouldn't want your teenage son to see. But besides his stated intentions, his nearness was having an effect on her that was becoming too familiar. He smelled so good, like soap and sunshine, that she almost relaxed for a minute, almost let her body melt against his.

"Did you and David straighten things out?" he asked, interrupting her thoughts.

"Yes. I'm grateful to you for arranging it," she answered. "How did you know that David was worrying?"

Hamp felt a flicker of annoyance. He didn't want Dani to feel grateful to him. That was the last emotion he wanted from her. He shrugged. "It wasn't hard to figure out. David is becoming a man, and he has a man's frustration at not being able to take care of his woman, even if the woman in question is his mother."

Dani couldn't believe what she was hearing. "That's archaic. David wouldn't feel like that."

"It's normal. I believe you just had a demonstration of how normal it is."

"It's demeaning," she countered.

"It's a perfectly natural masculine trait."

"Which I will discourage, natural or not." As she had just made very plain to her son, she didn't intend to lean on anyone. Maybe it was time to reinforce the idea in Hamp's case. Her anger simmered beneath the surface while she mulled over the outdated concept. At the end of the dance the band took a break. Grudgingly she admitted to herself that she felt chilled when Hamp dropped his arms. And she was doubly irritated with herself for feeling that way. This had to be stopped.

They approached the table. The sight of the youngsters brought her back to her senses. She put some steel in her backbone and a hand on Hamp's arm to slow his steps. "Hamp . . ." The other dancers, headed off the floor, circling them. "I don't know how to say this. . . ."

While Dani frowned, searching for the right words, Hamp's brief flicker of annoyance returned. Seconds ago he had felt anger stiffen the slender body he held, felt it and wasn't sure what he'd done to deserve it. "Why not try words?" he suggested mildly.

"I wouldn't want you to think I'm not grateful," she said again.

He lowered his voice to a growl. "Dammit, woman, I don't want your gratitude. If you're angry with yourself because I recognized David's feelings before you did, forget it. You would have realized what was bothering him eventually."

"I'm not angry with myself about that."

"Well, you've been behaving like a mule with an itch to scratch all night. Just spit it out."

A mule! "All right, I will. The kiss this morning, the long sultry looks, the little touches, the suggestive innuendo." She screwed up her face. "I want to hold you," she mimicked in a parody of his deep voice. "Among other things."

Suddenly Hamp's anger reached its full potential. No man likes to have his sexual advances made fun of—declined politely, but never ridiculed. "I didn't hear you complaining too loudly while you rubbed yourself against me in the *marae*," he said crudely. "And for your information—in case you don't recognize simple declarative sentence structure—that one isn't an innuendo. It's a flat-out statement."

Dani clamped her mouth shut and inhaled deeply, refusing to let him see how his words hit a sensitive spot deep within her. The coarse, suggestive remark was the least of it. Her aborted education had always been her sore spot, and however unknowingly, he had just struck that bruise with unnecessary force. "You're the professor," she snapped. "You put a name to it. Just remember, I'm not looking for a vacation fling and I have no intention of letting myself be seduced—*or* taken care of."

"Fine. Although I don't remember offering to take care of you, that's just fine with me," Hamp snapped back. "Maybe we should call off the shopping trip tomorrow."

Dani hesitated, overwhelmingly tempted by the suggestion. She would be better-off far, far away from this man.

Then she thought of Sandy. The child had accompanied them willingly to Huahine, trusting in their bargain. It would be cruel and possibly disastrous for her relationship with her father, to renege at this point.

"I don't give a damn whether we go or not, but you might not want to dismiss your daughter's expectations so easily.

Just let me know what you decide." She turned her back on him and strode out of the dining room.

Hamp stood alone on the edge of the dance floor, glaring after her and feeling ashamed. He rarely gave in to his temper. He prided himself on being controlled and clearheaded. But this had been a hell of a day, emotionally.

HAMP WAS THE FIRST one down to breakfast. David was second. Sandy and Dani arrived at the same time. Conversation around the table was comprised of nothing more interesting than "Pass the butter."

Dani presumed that Hamp was planning to go on with the shopping expedition, as he didn't say anything about calling it off.

There was nothing to do but put the best face possible on the situation, she decided. It would be a long day, but when it was over they could go their separate ways. After the scene last night, she was sure Hamp would be as relieved as she was at the prospect.

She glanced up from her pineapple juice to find his gaze on her, inscrutable as ever. She wished he would take off those damned glasses.

He drained his coffee cup. "Did you sleep well?" he asked mildly.

She set the juice down and touched the corner of her mouth with her napkin. "Yes, fine. And you?"

Instead of answering, Hamp nodded, looking down at the mess he'd left on his plate. "What time would you like to leave for Papeete?"

She checked her watch. "Does nine-thirty suit you?"

"Fine. If you'll excuse me, I have a couple of calls to make before we leave." He left.

"What's the matter with Daddy?" asked Sandy when he'd gone. "I thought he was having a good time, that he'd loosened up a little. But this morning he's downright morose."

Dani had hoped the youngsters would put the strained silence down to the late night they'd had. The circles under her eyes certainly were witness to it. "He's probably tired," she said. "I know I am."

5

THE FOUR MET in the lobby precisely at nine-thirty. They walked down the curving drive of the hotel and crossed the road to meet Le Truck, the open-air, wooden-paneled vehicle that would take them into the city. They had only been waiting for a few minutes when their transportation came careening around the curve, gears screeching, metal parts rattling and accelerator apparently stuck to the floorboard.

Hamp raised his hand. The driver gave them a snaggle-toothed grin and slammed on the brakes, coming to a stop about thirty yards beyond where they stood. They ran for the rear door. The seats, which ran parallel down each side, were filled but their fellow passengers cheerfully made space on the center wooden bench.

David squeezed in between a massive woman with a woven basket of fruit at her feet and a young beach-boy type with a ghetto blaster perched on his shoulder, its twin speakers wailing a Springsteen lament. A few feet down, Sandy turned to pat the head of a small pig, perched precariously on the lap of a wizened old man.

Dani and Hamp were at the end of the bench, by the open door. In the crowded bus there was no way to avoid bodily contact. He relaxed next to her, his large body adjusting naturally to the sway and movement. She could not help being conscious of his every shift, while he seemed totally unaware of her.

When the driver slammed on the brakes once again, David spoke around the fat lady. "I wonder if we get to hold this group in our laps?"

Hamp grinned at him and pointed upward. "There's a whole second story."

Sure enough, the three people who had been waiting scrambled up one of the outside ladders that flanked the back door onto the roof of the bus.

The ride took nearly forty-five minutes. By the time they arrived Dani's muscles were aching from the hard backless bench, the complete lack of springs in the vehicle and the struggle to hold herself aloof from the sensation of Hamp's warm body next to hers. She would have given a night's take at the club for the limousine.

Papeete was unquestionably urban, a once sleepy village transformed into a lively metropolis. Built around the harbor, it was crescent shaped with its streets running off the Boulevard Pomare like spokes of half a wheel. Here in the city, the Polynesian atmosphere had definitely been suppressed in favor of the French. Even in the naming of the streets the French had stamped their own mark—Rue du Général De Gaulle, Place Notre Dame, Rue Dumont D'Urville.

Le Truck deposited them in the center of town and from then on, for the rest of the morning, Sandy led the way. When, at one o'clock, the shops closed for a leisurely two-hour break, they were ready for a break, as well—or at least three of them were. They found themselves outside La Pizzeria Tahiti. David didn't even consult with the others; he led the way inside and collapsed in a chair. "Sandy, you have shopping down to a fine art," he said with a trace of admiration in his tone.

Sandy didn't even look wilted; she ignored the thrust. "Pizza in Papeete. I never dreamed we'd be so lucky."

"The city prides itself on its international cuisine, but this is ridiculous," muttered Hamp.

Two hours later, refreshed by a hearty Italian meal, they set out again. At the Tahitian Cultural Center they watched stone and wood sculptors, they cheered for the entry from Huahine in a canoe race in the harbor and, standing at the edge of a tour group, they listened to a lecture on the origin of the beautiful and mysterious black pearl of the South Seas.

By six o'clock they were hot, tired and thirsty. Rather than go all the way back to Maeva Beach they decided to stay in town for dinner. Sandy and David began a debate on the relative merits of Mexican food versus German food.

Dani met Hamp's eyes in amused tolerance. Since their argument yesterday, the two young people had rarely agreed on anything. But unlike yesterday, their wrangling held subdued good humor.

Dani found a bench beneath a large shade tree and sat down to wait for them to make up their minds.

Finally Hamp shifted the packages he held to one arm and fished in the back pocket of his chinos. Out came a brochure that he slapped into David's hand.

"Here's a map of the city with all the restaurants listed. You have your choice of Chinese, French, Japanese, Vietnamese, Polynesian, French and a few dozen more. Just let us know when you decide," he said and joined Dani on the bench. "And no pizza," he added, looking to her for confirmation.

"No pizza," she agreed.

He sighed and stretched his long legs out in front of him, crossing them at the ankle.

Dani smiled tentatively; he returned it. They had stayed a part of the group today, evading any opportunity to be alone. They had been polite but distant, which was the way it had to be, she told herself repeatedly. After today they would not see each other again, except in the most casual way. She wasn't sure whether she wanted to feel relief or sadness at the thought, so she put her emotions on hold, enjoying only the minute.

"It's been a nice day," she ventured.

"Yes, it has. I would have gotten a lot more out of it, though, if I hadn't acted like such an ass last night." He put a hand up to massage his neck.

Dani laughed softly and wiggled her toes around the straps of her sandals. "Me, too. It's a shame we're so different."

Hamp opened his mouth to say something else but before he could speak the youngsters came to stand in front of them. "We've decided on Polynesian-style ribs," Sandy announced, every bit as bright and cheerful as she'd been at nine-thirty that morning.

Wearily Dani dragged herself to her feet. "Fine. I just hope we don't have to walk too far for them."

In deference to the heat of the day they had worn loose, casual clothes. Sandy was dressed in baggy clam-digger pants and an oversize shirt, Hamp and David in short-sleeved shirts, Dani in a cool green sundress.

The restaurant they had chosen was small, on a side street, away from the hustle and noise of traffic. Like most of the bars and restaurants in Tahiti, it was open to the evening air. Scents of plumeria and frangipani mingled with the dusty smell of the city streets and the wonderful, scintillating odors from the kitchen that made Dani's mouth water.

An island band played island music, and Hamp and Dani each ordered an island drink recommended by the waiter as the house speciality. Some kind of local fermented wine mixed with fruit juices, it was delivered in an extra tall glass

that was wonderfully frosty. David ordered Coca-Cola;
Sandy, a Pepsi.

They devoured the greasy ribs, along with fruit salad,
baked yams and a lighter-than-air lemon soufflé.

After dinner the music grew louder and more lively. The
small restaurant-club didn't cater particularly to tourists,
but there were a few in addition to themselves. Business
women and men also drifted in, loosening ties and shed-
ding jackets as they came. Relaxing from a hard day at work
in paradise, thought Dani.

Soon a group of Tahitian dancers appeared and, after
finishing their performance to loud applause and whistles,
came into the audience to draft participants.

When one of the male dancers approached her, Dani
shook her head. Suddenly his figure was wavy and slightly
blurred. Not until that moment had Dani realized how potent the drinks were. She was feeling the effects after sip-
ping only half of her first one.

But Hamp had had two. The third was sitting in front of
him, untouched. And his smile was slightly awry as he responded to the beckoning gesture of a dancer. The woman
was tall and exquisitely built, with a waist-length mane of
hair as black as the night. Her skirt, made of dried grass with
a wide, woven girdle embellished with dangling shells, sat
low on her hips. A bra of flowered material barely covered
her breasts, and on her head she wore the traditional *hei
upo'o*, a crown of flowers.

The beat of the music was heavy, sensual. Hamp followed the woman onto the dance floor; she turned to face
him, a smoky, seductive smile on her lips. She put her hands
on his sides, just below his belt, indicating which way she
wanted him to move, while her own hips moved in a coun-
terrhythm, slowly at first, gaining speed and agility as the
music picked up its tempo.

Hamp's lean body gyrated in perfect time to the beat. He must have done this before. And he wasn't bad at it despite the fermented wine, thought Dani, swallowing against a sudden dryness in her mouth.

"Daddy's going to have a beauty of a hangover in the morning," said Sandy wryly.

Dani tore her eyes away from the spectacle in front of her to look at the youngster. She wondered if Sandy disapproved; she seemed to be relishing the sight of her father letting his hair down, but you never knew. "Does he do this sort of thing often?" she asked.

"Never. That's why it's so funny. I'm always trying to get him to loosen up."

The speed of the dance had begun to accelerate rapidly now. His partner was a born flirt, her own hips rotating faster and faster, until they were almost a blur. Hands in the air, their bodies brushed, separated. The natural grasses of the dancer's skirt swished, showing glimpses of rounded thighs as she edged closer... and closer, her smile one of clear and open invitation.

Dani stared, openmouthed. The dance was the most erotic thing she had ever seen.

Finally the music ended in a flourishing crescendo of drums. Dani slumped in her chair, utterly drained.

Hamp returned to his seat, grinning broadly and barely breathing hard from the exertion. A thin film of perspiration glistened on his brow, however, and he brushed it away with the flat of his hand, which he then dried on his pants leg.

As Dani watched in horror he reached for his drink and upended it, swallowing thirstily, draining the glass, before putting it down with a thump. "That was fun," he said. "You ought to try it, Danielle."

Danielle? Good grief.

He stood up again, not quite steady, and grabbed her hand. "C'mon. I'll show you."

It wasn't difficult to change his mind. All she had to do was give a sharp jerk of his hand and he flopped back down in his chair. "No," she said with finality.

"Spoilsport," he muttered.

Dani reacted with amusement. "Hamp Lowell, you have had too much to drink." Realizing that she was the only rational adult present, she decided on a course of action. She turned to the children. "I think we'd better get him back to the hotel while he can still walk."

David sighed, looking disappointed, but he didn't say anything. Sandy voiced her own chagrin eloquently enough for both of them. "Leave? We just got here." She looked down at her watch. "It's only eight-thirty, Dani. Please, can't we stay just for a little while longer?" she pleaded, her eyes traveling from one adult to the other.

Dani hesitated. Hamp was a grown man, responsible for his own actions. She glanced at him. He tilted his head slightly to the side. Looking like a small boy about to be chastened, he raised both brows and smiled expectantly. "This wine is potent, isn't it? I'm afraid you're right. I'd like to go back to the hotel."

Though Dani struggled to keep a straight face, she was enjoying this. "You would?"

"Yes. Will you go with me?" he asked on a plaintive note. Both kids were trying to keep from smiling.

"What about Sandy and David? They want to stay."

"They can stay. I consider David totally trustworthy," he said, throwing his arm around David's shoulder in a magnanimous gesture. "He'll take care of my little girl as well as I would myself."

David's smile wavered somewhat, but he nodded. "I'll stay with her," he said.

"Now, wait just a da-darn minute." Sandy glanced quickly at her father to see if he noticed the near slip, but he was blissfully unaware. "I don't need a baby-sitter," she went on with her protest.

Bless David, thought Dani, when her son replied easily, "Of course you don't, squirt. I'm an escort, not a sitter. There's a difference, you know."

Sandy subsided without any further retort, probably grasping at last that she would stay with David or she would not stay at all.

"You two behave yourselves," Dani directed as she and Hamp stood to leave. She gathered up two packages along with her purse. "And don't stay out too late. Do you have money for a taxi?"

"Yes," David assured her. "Don't worry, Mom. And I'll get the rest of this stuff." He indicated the remaining bags. "See you in the morning. Night, Professor."

"Good night, David. Sandy, would you please call me when you get in?"

Hamp had reverted suddenly to parental formality. A little late for that, thought Dani.

"Yes, Daddy," said Sandy, then spoiled it by giggling.

They stepped onto the sidewalk and Dani looked around for a cab. She saw one at the end of the next block. When a wave didn't catch the driver's attention, she put two fingers to her lips and let loose an earsplitting whistle.

"Good grief, woman," complained Hamp, putting both hands over his ears. The echo seemed to be bouncing around inside his brain. "Where the hell did you learn to do that?"

"From my husband. He taught me a lot of useful things," she said, and marched over to meet the circling taxi.

Hamp watched her sassy behind as she pranced across the narrow street. He wasn't as badly off as he'd let Dani be-

lieve, but he wasn't totally sober, either. The trouble with
that stuff was that it seemed to recur. One minute he felt as
sober as a judge—almost. The next he'd feel the silly grin
spreading across his face and a pleasant fog befuddling his
senses. He decided that the worst of the wine's effect occurred when he relaxed.

Shaking his head in an attempt to clear it, he tried to recall his motives for leaving the club. He'd had a plan; now
what was it? If it hadn't been so damned hot, if he hadn't
been so damned thirsty, he wouldn't be in this damned condition. So much for originality, he rebuked himself.

"I hope you have some money," she threw back over her
shoulder. "I spent all my cash today."

"Yeah, I have money," he informed her. He held on to the
door more than he held it for her, but at last they were in
the taxi. "The Maeva Beach Hotel," he told the driver, raising his voice to be heard over the noise of the radio blasting
out rock music. He slumped in the seat. "It's been a long
day," he observed.

She didn't comment.

He turned toward her. "Dani," he began, then stopped to
glare at the back of the driver's head. "Could you turn that
down, please?"

The driver lowered the volume half a decibel.

"Dani," he began again, more precisely. "I want you to
know that this sort of behavior is not my usual style."

"I should hope not," she answered, keeping her eyes
averted, her face straight ahead. He had to bend closer to
hear her over the still-loud radio.

"I want to apologize for subjecting you to—I mean—I
have a drink occasionally, but I don't get—" he searched for
an appropriate word; the fermented wine recurred "—fuzzy-
wuzzy." Damn!

She bit her lips, hard. "Fuzzy-wuzzy?" she said after a minute. "How descriptive."

He shrugged. "I'm not at my best."

"Obviously. Look, Hamp, don't worry about it, okay? In my line of work I've had to deal with drunks before. Believe me, you're not as bad as some."

His jaw went slack. "Drunks?" he asked, disbelieving. "You think I'm drunk?"

He sounded terribly offended, and Dani decided she'd better back up. "Well, as I said, I've seen worse."

"Look, Danielle. I may be a little high, but I—am—not—drunk." He folded his arms across his broad chest. "And I don't appreciate your insinuation that I am."

"Whatever," she said dismissively.

"Good, I'm glad we understand each other." He was beginning to develop a bitch of a headache.

Dani shot him a look.

He leaned back in the seat and closed his eyes. He'd rest them for a minute.

The remainder of the ride passed in silence and when they reached the hotel she understood why. Not until the driver switched off his motor could she hear that Hamp was snoring softly. His glasses were tilted, slightly askew on the bridge of his nose.

She resisted the temptation to slip them off and hide them from him.

Leaning forward to look up at the front of the hotel, she was relieved to see that the doorman was not at his post and through the wide double doors the lobby appeared to be deserted. Although why she should feel relief was beyond her. What did it matter to her if the professor chose to make an absolute fool of himself? Using her elbow she nudged him. "Hamp, we're here."

He was slow to awaken, but he followed her when she climbed out of the taxi. He propped on the right rear bumper and closed his eyes again.

"I need your money, Hamp," she said.

"Mmm?"

Taking a deep breath, she dug into his pocket for his money clip. He opened his eyes, straightened his glasses and smiled at her. "I like that," he drawled.

Dani rolled her eyes in exasperation, removed a bill and thrust it at the driver before jamming the clip back into his pocket.

"Do you need some help getting him inside, lady?" the cabbie offered.

She regarded her charge warily. His eyes were still open; she supposed that was a hopeful sign. However, he also wore that insipid smile. "I think I can manage. Thanks," she said, draping Hamp's arm over her shoulder. Not for support—she could never support his weight—but to steer him in the right direction. There were four shallow but broad steps to be traversed. And by the time they had climbed them Dani was breathing hard. Thank heavens, she noted, the front desk was deserted.

"Hey, lady!"

She swiveled her head. The taxi driver was bounding up the steps.

"Your packages," he called.

"Thanks a lot!" she exclaimed, taking them in the hand that was behind Hamp's back.

Hamp nuzzled her temple with little hungry kisses. "You're so pretty." With his hand he rubbed her arm, down and back up, in a warming movement, as though they were in the Arctic rather than practically sitting on the equator.

Catching his fingers she linked them with her own to keep them still. "Thank you," she muttered.

"And sexy, too. Did you know you are sexy, Danielle?"

"Hamp." She made two syllables of his name.

"I'm trying to avoid innuendo tonight. So I'm just saying what I think."

"You're going to hate yourself in the morning." They took a few more steps. A man came out of a door behind the desk, dressed in the natty gold blazer worn by the hotel staff. Dani smiled, gave a casual wave and continued walking.

The desk clerk waved back. "Have a nice evening," he said in a heavily accented basso.

"Thank you," answered Dani.

"We had a lovely evening," explained Hamp. "Now we're going to bed," he announced cheerfully.

Dani's gaze followed the desk clerk's to the large carved clock on the wall. Nine-fifteen. Most of the guests had just gone down to dinner.

"Good night," replied the man with a knowing smile.

"I ought to dump you right here," grated Dani when they had passed out of his line of vision.

"Please don't."

She had a thought. "Hamp, what is your room number?" She knew it was on this floor and down this hall, but she had no idea which room it was.

"Two-one-two." He frowned. "Or is it two-two-one? Never mind. It's on the key and the key's in my pocket."

She sighed her impatience. "Well, would you get it out and look at it, please?"

His eyes gleamed when he grinned down at her. "Are you sure you don't want to fish around in there for it. I kind of enjoyed—"

Unlinking their fingers she slapped her hand over his mouth, muffling his words. The elevator had stopped as they were passing. Two couples had emerged and were watching them interestedly.

"Don't even think that, Hampton Lowell the Third. Do you understand? Just hand me the damned key."

He complied meekly, digging into the pocket.

"I want some coffee. Let's go to the coffee shop."

"No," she replied. "If you want coffee you can order it from room service."

"Will you have some with me?"

"No." She found the room. It was two-one-two. She inserted the key and opened the door. "Good night," she said, guiding him forward.

Hamp didn't let go his hold. He looked down at her lips, which were pursed in a sexy little pout. They looked tempting, but he was sober enough to know that if he said so she'd be out of here like a shot. "You're mad at me," he said sadly.

"No, Hamp. I'm not mad at you." She answered his accusation with what, for her, was great forbearance.

"Then why won't you stay for a cup of coffee? It won't take long. I ordered some last night and they were here in— oh—five minutes. Tops. I really need that coffee, Dani."

"That's the truest thing you've said tonight." Dani inhaled and let the air out slowly. "All right. One cup of coffee. Do you want me to call?"

"No, I can do it."

And he did, in a surprisingly sober voice. Dani's eyes narrowed on him, until he flopped back on the bed and grinned lopsidedly again. "Come sit here beside me." He patted the mattress next to his hip.

"No, I'll be very comfortable here." She sat down in a chair and crossed her legs.

He eyed them appreciatively. They were long and sleek and smooth. "Aw, Dani. I'm not going to attack you."

"I didn't think you were," she said calmly, not missing his appraisal.

Hamp's head was beginning to clear. He searched for an innocuous topic of conversation, realizing that he needed to get his mind off how sexy she was, how pretty and tasty her lips looked. He pulled out a pillow and stuffed it behind the small of his back, as he had done on her bed, shifting until he was comfortable. "Tell me about your club. If I'm not mistaken, it used to be called something else. How did you end up as the owner?"

Dani hadn't expected the question, but decided it was as good a subject as any. "The club was called Happy Isle."

"That's right, I remember. It didn't used to be as nice a place as it is now."

Dani laughed reminiscently. "It was a dump. The owner's name was Schyler. He was a nice enough man, but had no business sense. Two years after I went to work there he let me buy into a partnership. When he retired I borrowed the money to buy him out, took over completely and re-named the place." Her eyes took on a faraway look. The simple statement didn't begin to describe a young woman's terrible fears—fear of being alone, fear of some of the rougher clientele, fear that Schyler, plagued by financial problems, would sell to someone else before she could scrape up the money for a partnership.

Davey had left them a small insurance policy—not enough, but a beginning. She'd known that she couldn't bring up her son properly without stability in their lives. With the responsibility of part ownership, her fears had taken a different direction. Every improvement, every change, had been fought for over Schyler's stubborn objections. She sighed.

Watching her expression, Hamp filled in the gaps for himself, wishing he'd known her then. He, too, looked

back. At the time she was buying a partnership in a sec-
ond-rate club, struggling to establish a life for herself and
her son, he was praying that the birth of his daughter would
straighten out his marriage.

"You don't look comfortable," he said, lurching slightly
as he got to his feet. He came to her side, and before she realized what his intentions were, he'd scooped her up and
returned to the bed. "There." He laid her on the spot he'd
vacated. He placed his hands on either side of her and
grinned. The grin was boyish and appealing, intended to
remove the threat from her position.

The bed beneath her was warm from his body, but she
resisted the temptation to relax into the heat. "Hamp," she
said, deliberately accenting the warning in her voice.

He straightened. With his fists planted on his lean hips he
lifted a brow. "If you'll scoot over, I'll join you."

Dani scooted, as far to the other side as she could get.
Hamp arranged his long form parallel to hers, but he didn't
touch her. He laced his fingers behind his head and sighed.
The pose stretched the blue knit shirt over his broad chest.
Dani had a sudden and inexplicable urge to rest her head
there. It was that kind of chest. She battled the impulse.

They were quiet for a minute. "You're going to hate
yourself in the morning, you know," she said softly.

"You said that." He turned on his side to face her and bent
his elbow, resting his head on his hand. "Maybe I will, but
I don't think so," he said seriously. He tucked a strand of her
hair behind her ear, letting his fingers linger on her soft skin.
"You feel like silk."

She turned her face away. "Hamp, don't," she whispered. "We don't even like each other. Look at the way we
argued last night."

"On the contrary, I like you too much," he said huskily, but he withdrew his hand. "Too damned much. I didn't sleep worth a damn. Did you?"

"Not particularly well, no," she admitted. She waited, holding her breath, somehow knowing what was coming. And somehow needing to hear the words, though not wanting to hear them.

"I want you, Dani, want you so desperately that it's eating a hole in my gut."

She closed her eyes. "It's the fermented wine talking."

Hamp watched the heavy lashes shadow her cheeks. "No." Tread lightly, he cautioned himself. "No, it isn't the wine, though it had its effect."

Dani laughed. "I know. I felt it, too." She hesitated, then reached over and removed his glasses. He made no protest. She searched his features, seeing there what she had seen in her own mirror and refused to acknowledge. Shaking her head she started to replace them, but Hamp took them from her and folded them. He reached behind his head to lay them on the table beside the bed. "I don't need my glasses when we're this close," he said.

She frowned slightly, then she sat up and wrapped her arms around her knees. "It would never work, Hamp. I'm not prone to one-night affairs."

Annoyance surfaced. That she could make such a judgment of his motives irked him. "Neither am I, dammit!" He pulled her down beside him, more roughly than he should have.

Her face, her body, froze.

He released her immediately and stared down into her eyes. "Neither am I," he repeated, more softly now. "I definitely want more than one night with you."

Slowly he lowered his head. He wasn't holding her; she could have escaped at any time. He was giving her plenty of room. He wasn't forcing her. All these things ricocheted through her mind, setting up little warning flares each time they encountered her pragmatic streak. And she lay motionless for a breathless moment, waiting for him to kiss her.

Again, as with the first kiss, his lips were warm and sure. His mouth moved over hers, mobile and hungry, and yet this kiss carried more promise than passion. He knew, they knew, that tonight wasn't the right time. She responded, equally confident, despite the unfamiliar heat that coursed through every vein, carried along by an accelerated pulse. He kissed her and withdrew, kissed her again and withdrew again.

She sighed and lay her hand on his cheek. Against her lips he smiled that half smile she liked. "Do I taste as good to you as you do to me?" he asked gently, tenderly, his breath, slightly flavored with wine, warm in her mouth.

"Yes," she whispered, nodding her head. The action loosened the twist of hair at her nape and she felt a hairpin dig into her flesh. "Ouch."

"Here, let me," he said. Turning her toward him, he pulled out the remaining pins and tossed them aside. He massaged the injured spot and combed her hair with his fingers. "This was the first thing I noticed about you," he murmured, sweeping her hair aside and settling his lips on her bare shoulder.

Shivery, sparkling ribbons of brilliance radiated out from his lips, climbing her scalp, slithering down her spine. Maybe she needed this. Maybe she needed to be made love to, hungrily, passionately. Maybe it would ease the restlessness in her. Her lips were on a level with his jaw. On impulse she touched him there with her tongue and felt his response. Immediately caution took over; she pulled back. "Hair is the first thing anyone notices about a redhead. But

we learn to live with that," she quipped somewhat breath-
lessly.

"Come back here. You can't nibble at my chin and then
pull away." He settled her closer in his arms. "I wouldn't
describe your hair as red. I'd say it was a flame, a blaze or
maybe a sunset. Never merely red."

"It's the same color as the bolts on Jonny's plane. Rusty.
Was I nibbling?" she asked. He chuckled, the sound vi-
brating through her.

"We seem to be discussing two different topics. Let's toss
them and pick up the other one."

"Which other one?"

He cradled her chin in his big hand. "The one about
making love to each other."

His hair had fallen forward over his forehead. Dani
combed it back with her fingers. It was an affectionate gesture. He inhaled sharply.

Dani pulled away and swung her feet over the edge of the
bed. "Oh, hell, this isn't going to work."

He had realized from the first kiss, shared in the *marae*,
that she wasn't going to have as simple an effect on him as
most of the women he knew. Now she was showing an unexpected tenderness. He hadn't seen that in her before. "Let's
talk it over."

"I don't think so, Hamp." She smiled, but her heart wasn't
in it. She rose from the bed, combing her hair back with her
fingers, and slid her hands down the front of her dress in an
attempt to level some of the creases. It didn't work. She
shrugged. "I think it's best if I run along now. I'll see you tomorrow, probably."

A knock on the door startled them both.

"The coffee," Hamp murmured unnecessarily. He reached
for his glasses. Raking his hair back from his forehead, he
went to the door to admit the waiter. The man smiled me-

chanically as he set the small tray on the dresser and held
out a check to Hamp, who scribbled his name at the bottom.

Picking up her purse and packages, Dani started to follow him out, but was stopped by Hamp's voice.

"Dani."

She turned, ready to defend her decision with a polite
smile. He stood, feet apart, hands on his hips. His clothes
were as wrinkled as hers, his eyes as wary and defensive. He
looked tired, she thought, mildly surprised. He didn't look
like the type of man who ever let his weariness—or any kind
of weakness—show.

"At least have a cup of coffee with me since it's here.
Please."

Her resolve wavered. "All right." She lifted the strap off
her shoulder and let the bag slide to the floor. The paper
bags rustled. "Will you pour, or shall I?" she said lightly.

He turned away. "You do it. My hands seem to be shaking. I could hardly sign the check."

She decided it would be wisest not to comment on that
remark as she reached for the pot. She heard the sliding door
move on its tracks. Unlike hers, it opened instead onto a
narrow balcony, but the view was the same. Scents both
floral and tropical flooded the room with freshness from the
night air.

"That's much better than air-conditioning," she said as
she filled the two cups with coffee. Her hands were steady,
she noted with pride, steadier than her voice. "Do you take
cream and sugar?"

"Black."

When he didn't turn, she filled his cup and set it on the
table. "The hotel has wonderful coffee," she said. Small talk.

"Usually, if I come to the islands alone, I rent or borrow
a small sloop and camp out on a *motu*."

The information surprised her. The *motus*, she knew, were the small flat islands, similar to the barrier islands off the east coast of the United States, that had built up over centuries on a base of coral reef. The larger ones were sometimes used for cultivation, but more often were left deserted, low strips of sand dotted with palms, offering some protection when the elements became angry at paradise. Most of the lagoons were ringed with them.

How quickly one's perceptions of people could change, mused Dani. If she'd been asked what this man liked to do when she first met him, camping would have been at the bottom of the list. Until she'd become familiar with the different facets of his character, he'd appeared one-dimensional—a college professor with formal, if exquisite, tastes. Now that she'd seen him in other situations—as a concerned parent, as an almost-lover—she realized how much her concept of his personality had broadened.

"What are you thinking?" he asked sharply.

Startled by the tone of his voice, she looked up. He had pivoted slightly to rest his shoulder against the jamb. She wondered how long he had been watching her. "About stereotypes," she answered lightly. "What's it like to camp on a deserted island?"

"Have you ever camped?"

"Not since my husband died. He liked the desert."

As Hamp watched, Dani's eyes again took on a faraway look, shutting him out. He was surprised at his reaction. Jealousy was an unfamiliar emotion to him.

She shrugged and let go of the picture, whatever it was. "It's been years. But I used to enjoy it," she said, as though she'd just realized how much. "The sky was so big, and it was very quiet."

He turned back to stare unseeingly into the blackness. When he spoke his voice was low and soft. "Out there it's quiet, too, most of the time. The waves break on the ocean side and occasionally you'll hear a coconut drop. But at the edge of the lagoon, the waves whisper with a soft voice, of things to know, to find out. They beckon, like the Sirens. It's like sitting on the end of the world, waiting. Just waiting."

Dani knew intuitively that these were feelings he usually kept suppressed. Adding "poet" to her list of things she was learning about him, she felt as though she'd been given a look into the inner man.

All at once she shivered, preferring him to be guarded as he usually was. He was less dangerous when he was guarded. "It sounds lonely."

"I've never equated solitude with loneliness." Hamp shook himself mentally, realizing that he had revealed more of himself than he'd planned to. Surprisingly he didn't regret it. He came back into the room and reached for his coffee cup. "I prefer camping, but I couldn't ask Sandy to— What are you laughing about?"

"I'm trying to picture Sandy camping out." She picked up the responsive laughter in his eyes with some relief and sipped her coffee, which was heavily laced with cream and sugar. She placed the spoon in the saucer and mused silently for a moment. "Though she would probably adjust better than you'd expect."

"My Sandy?" he scoffed and drank from his cup.

She nodded and settled back into the chair. "A minute ago you asked what I was thinking. And I answered that I was thinking about stereotypes. I believe it's a mistake to try to fit someone into a category. Sandy, for instance."

He inspected her face for irony, but found none there. "I've been considering the same thing," he admitted. "You, for instance."

She lifted an eyebrow, but didn't speak, waiting for him to go on.

"I thought I had you pegged. You owned a nightclub; that can't be an easy business."

She nodded, giving him that.

"I figured you for one tough lady. Even when you were afraid to fly, I decided that was about the only thing you were afraid of." He paused, took a breath. "You are astonishingly beautiful. I believed you were reasonably experienced." When she started to protest both the beauty and the experience, he held up a hand. "Let me finish before you jump down my neck. At that *marae*? There was no restraint in the way you responded to that kiss."

She subsided, nodding again, but this time unwillingly. She knew he was right; she didn't have to like it. She took a swallow of coffee.

"My first marriage was a disaster from the beginning."

Dani blinked. As he had a tendency to do, he had switched subjects on her. Or had he?

"We were too pretty nice people who married for all the wrong reasons. By the time we divorced we had become two not-very-nice people. But I would have stayed with Miriam. I believe in vows and I had taken a vow to love and honor. The divorce hurt me more than it did her. So I made another vow: not to get involved emotionally again.

"I want you, Dani, more than I've wanted any woman for years. But I have to tell you that whatever our relationship becomes, I will never marry again."

The speech should have sounded arrogant, but it didn't. She smiled, genuinely and with relief. "Hamp, I appreciate your honesty, really I do. But this conversation is unnecessary. Although I'm attracted to you, ah, in an intimate way, I'm not interested in marriage, either. I've worked too hard to build my own independence to be able to consider another person in my plans and decisions. I'm afraid I'm too selfish."

"Then would you consider coming to Huahine with us for the rest of your vacation?"

Dani couldn't hide her shock at the totally unexpected question. "Why?" she breathed.

"To spend some more time together. To explore our feelings. Maybe to make love." He gave a deprecating shrug. "If the occasion arises, which it probably won't with two kids dogging our heels, and if we both agree that's what we want."

She looked at him warily. "I'll have to think about that for a while."

"You don't even have to come with us tomorrow. You could wait a day or two and fly over on an Air Polynesia flight." He smiled and set down his empty cup. "Though Jonny would be deeply offended at me for saying this, their planes don't have rust spots."

She wavered. "We both recognize that the relationship has to be temporary." It was not quite a statement, not quite a question.

"Of course."

"David would enjoy it."

Hamp tamped his irritation. Why did she have to rationalize? Why couldn't she come because she wanted to be with him? "And I would enjoy having him with me, to share the work I have to accomplish while we're there. He might even get some extra credit out of it," he added to sweeten the bait, then wished he hadn't.

She tilted her head a bit. "Are you trying to give me a sensible excuse for accepting—if I decide to accept?"

Impatiently Hamp picked up the pot and sloshed coffee into his cup. "Hell, no. If you have to have a roll call of excuses, then you shouldn't come."

Dani digested that theory for a minute. She nodded. "You're right. If I have to think about it, I probably shouldn't." She gathered up her purse and packages and went to the door.

Hamp watched her. He wouldn't ask. "Well?" he said impetuously.

"I'll let you know in the morning."

6

WHAT CAN IT HURT? thought Dani later as she lay in her bed staring at the ceiling. She didn't have to ask to know that David would jump at the idea of spending the rest of their vacation on Huahine. She had witnessed his avid interest in an excavation near the hotel. The beaches were lovely, and not as crowded. The hotel itself was delightful, more like what she had envisioned when she and David had planned the trip.

Those were the pluses. Now she considered the minuses. The only one she could come up with, she dismissed immediately: the danger of becoming too emotionally involved with Hamp.

Explore their feelings, he had said. She liked the idea—not rushing into anything, not becoming victims of their own desire, just being together, thinking about it for a while. Aside from his sensual appeal, which was certainly there, she liked Hamp, really liked him, and she knew, without any egoism, that he liked her. Now that they had cleared the air, neither of them would make the mistake of believing this was more of a relationship than what it was. The kids would be a ready barrier to any careless mistakes they might be tempted to make.

Like tonight. Tonight had left her with a small but persistent ache in the pit of her stomach. If—and it was a big if—they decided to make love, it would be an intelligent choice, made mutually, after much thought.

If that were true, why didn't this ache go away?

She'd meant it when she told him she wasn't interested in sharing her life. Soon David would be an adult—legally he was already one—and soon she would have more time for herself. Not that she had ever begrudged the effort it took to bring him up as she felt Davey would have wanted. But she was also looking forward to a certain amount of freedom in her own life. Why would she want to sacrifice that liberty? She answered her own question. She wouldn't. Getting involved meant having to answer to someone else; having to care.

Here Dani paused in her thinking, reluctant to continue. A shudder ran through her, quickly, like a child running down a hillside; but she recovered immediately and finished the thought. Getting involved meant leaving yourself open to heartbreak. Oh, to hell with euphemisms. She had never been less than honest with herself. *Loving* was the word she'd avoided for years and would continue to avoid. Loving someone could lead straight to disaster.

Well, she didn't intend to fall in love with Hamp, she'd just spend a few days with him, enjoying some pleasant male companionship.

AT NOON the next day the foursome boarded Jonny's plane. The additional weight of their luggage just might be the proverbial straw, thought Dani as she strapped herself in and reached for Sandy's headphones.

Travis's Jeep awaited them at the airstrip and they climbed in for the trip to the hotel. As soon as they had unpacked their bags and changed into swimsuits, they rented snorkeling gear and headed for the lagoon visible from the lobby.

Dani watched her son as he expertly donned his mask, set the mouthpiece between his teeth and submerged himself not far from where Hamp was already swimming. Any remaining doubts about the wisdom of her decision had faded completely with David's reaction at breakfast to her announcement.

Thrilled was too mild a word and this was, after all, his vacation, his graduation present. Though she hadn't made up her mind wholly on that basis, she was pleased for David to have the opportunity to be here on this island with a man he admired so much.

"Come on, Dani," shouted Sandy. Her small feet looked lost in the huge flippers. "Last one in is you-know-what."

Dani worked at the stubborn strap of her mask as she walked, or waddled, into the water. Tiny colorful fish investigated her ankles.

Her first dip beneath the surface swamped her mask. She came up sputtering in chest-deep water. The dratted thing was still too loose. Emptying the mask, she pulled at the strap again, catching a strand of her hair in the metal teeth of the buckle. "Damn," she muttered to herself. "I'm going to go punk like Sandy with this mop as soon as I get home."

"With those little spikes sticking up all over your head? I hope not." Hamp had come out of the water beside her. "I would have to hire a plane and fly you around for days if you did that."

"That's a terrible thing to threaten me with. I'm not so sure I like you knowing my weakness."

Smiling, he pushed his mask, specially made with his prescription in the glass, to the top of his head. "Here, hold this." He handed her his snorkel tube and went to work on the strap. "Your hair is beautiful. It suits you."

The compliment unsettled her, along with the droplets of water clinging to the silky hair on his broad chest. She lifted her chin and came back with a quick rejoinder. "I'd think you'd want me to cut it all off. Every time I get too close to you, it seems to get in the way."

Hamp's hands stilled. He bent forward to see Dani's face. She had caught her lower lip between her white teeth. Her light green eyes sparkled with chagrin. "Sorry," she murmured around her smile.

"I should hope so." He smiled, too—a slow, lazy smile, knowing they shared the memory of the scene in his room, knowing that she was affected by the memory. "I think I can tolerate your hair, just barely, mind you, as long as I can anticipate seeing it spread out on my pillow again."

"You're incorrigible." She shook her head and laughed up into his eyes. "Hamp—the mask," she reminded.

He went back to his task. Working carefully so as not to hurt her, he finally managed to untangle the strap. "I have an idea. Why don't I make you a pigtail?"

She looked dubious. "Can you?"

"Sure." He handed her the mask to hold. "I had a little girl once. I'm good at pigtails." He looked out to where the kids were swimming, visible only by the small tubes extending above the water and an occasional splash when they kicked. She thought she saw longing in his eyes, but if it was there, it disappeared in an instant.

Taking her hair in his hands he squeezed out some of the water; then, efficiently, he separated the strands and began to braid.

Hamp's hands in her hair were having an odd effect on her equilibrium. Trying to tell herself it was the gentle motion of the water, she put a light hand on his arm for balance. She felt the muscles stiffen under her fingers and withdrew. "I don't have anything to tie it with," she told him.

"I'll get something. Hold this."

Now, in addition to both snorkels and her mask, she had the tail of her braid in her hands. She juggled to retain her grip on everything. "Do you have anything else you want me to hold, Professor?" she asked, grumbling.

He had been fishing around with his hands under the water. At her words he straightened abruptly and spun around, fixing her with a gaze that was suddenly hot and very hungry. "Yeah," he murmured. "I certainly do."

A word, a look, and suddenly the teasing went out of the moment. Dani couldn't move; she couldn't breathe. She was well and truly caught in the net of his sensuality. He came forward until he stood only inches, only millimeters from her. The heat from his body surrounded her until she felt as fluctuant and unstable as the water around them. Her gaze dropped to his mouth.

A soft groan escaped from somewhere deep in his chest. He took one step, reached for her, wrapping her arms, the equipment she held, her whole body close to him. His head came down to blot out the sun and a large hand slid below the level of the water to the base of her spine, pressing her hips to his hard thighs.

Dani didn't spare a thought for the few people on the beach or for David, or Sandy. Nor did she feel a moment's regret. Despite her own denials, she was where she wanted to be. She simply surrendered to her senses, now whirling out of control, feeling the physical evidence of his arousal. Her lips parted; her tongue met his.

From out of the haze that surrounded them she heard a familiar sound—something she ought to think about—but she was too disoriented to analyze the noise. Hamp raised his head just a fraction, not breaking contact with her lips. "I guess you taught him to do that," he murmured, his hoarse voice echoing her frustration.

"What?" Then she realized the sound was a whistle, shrill and piercing. "Oh, no." She rested her forehead against his chin. "Why did I ever do such a stupid thing?" she asked herself aloud.

Chuckling, he gave her one more quick, hard kiss and released her. "It's a good thing I'm waist deep in water." His dark eyes spoke more articulately than his husky voice.

"Yes."

He looked at her for a moment, gratified to see that her green eyes were dark now with desire, that she was as aroused as he. Wordlessly he took the braid from her unresisting fingers and fastened it with a piece of seaweed. Patiently he showed her how to spit in her mask to clear it, then he took his mouthpiece from her and waited while she adjusted hers between her swollen lips. "Are you ready?" he asked.

Her eyes flew to his.

"Oh, hell. Let's go. I hope the water's colder at the bottom."

"HEY, MOM." David caught up with her on the way to their cabin to change for dinner.

"Hi, honey."

"Mom," he said hesitantly as he matched his step to hers. "I hope I didn't do anything, uh, wrong this morning."

She knew exactly what he was talking about, but she didn't know how to reply. "Wrong?"

"Yeah, you know, when I whistled. I hope I didn't embarrass you or anything."

Were her cheeks as hot as they felt? she wondered, hoping David would put it down to the sun. "No. Not really."

"Well, I mean, you guys looked like you were ready to go at it, hot and heavy."

"David!"

"Well, you did," he insisted defensively. "I don't object, but I didn't think you'd want half the people in the hotel looking on."

Dani shook her head in wonder. When she dressed for dinner, however, she wore a conservatively tailored silk shirt and raw silk slacks.

Later, in the buffet line, Hamp came up behind her. He placed a proprietary hand at the side of her waist. "Were you subjected to a lecture this afternoon on the proper behavior for parents?"

"Yes," she whispered quietly. "You, too?"

"Hell, yes. Little Miss Prim-and-Proper chewed me out good for making a spectacle of myself and you."

Dani chuckled at the thought of Sandy as Miss Prim-and-Proper.

"Funny thing, though," he added, stroking her side with an absent motion. She wished he'd stop. He seemed almost unaware of what he was doing, but his touch was having a profound effect on her.

She caught his hand with hers to hold it still and look over her shoulder. "What was funny about it?" she asked seriously. "They were right. We weren't at all discreet." To her surprise and relish he also had color in his cheeks that wasn't owing to the sun. "Why, Professor, you're actually blushing."

"So are you," he growled, giving her side a squeeze, then linking his fingers with hers. "That was what they disapproved of, you see. Not the kiss itself, but the public setting."

They shared a small smile. "That's nice to know, isn't it?" said Dani.

"It's damned dangerous for you, my lady. You're brave, here with so many people around, but you'd better watch out when I get you alone. You could find yourself ravished," he whispered with a mock threat.

A pirate, she decided; he would make a splendid pirate. "'Ravished,'" she said, letting the word roll around on her tongue, savoring it. "What a deliciously decadent sort of sound that has, Professor."

Leaving Hamp with a speculative expression, she accepted a plate from the hostess and moved forward to the attractive display of island foods.

DAVID AND SANDY went off with a group of teenagers they had met at dinner. Comfortable with the night, the atmosphere and themselves, Hamp and Dani took off their shoes and rolled up their slacks. They sauntered slowly, fingers interlaced, along the beach. Rhythmic native drums beat a slow cadence for their steps. The sun was low on the horizon, like a huge red ball of fire struggling to the last to keep from being swallowed up by the ocean.

"Let's sit for a while." A huge Pacific chestnut tree grew near the water's edge, its shallow roots spread out along the ground. Underneath its branches the evening shadows were deeper, giving them a semblance of privacy.

Hamp chose a spot on the sand, his back to the trunk, and drew her down between his legs so she could lean against his chest.

He didn't hold her; his forearms were propped on his bent knees. His legs, his arms, made a harbor for her, not a cage. But Dani braced herself upright for a minute, pondering the wisdom of yielding to the intimate position. Finally she compromised, turning slightly so that one shoulder rested on his chest.

When Hamp felt her relax, he sighed, a deep, deep sound of utter contentment. "This time of day is what I like best about these islands. And this is the island I like best."

It was wonderful to share an ordinary sunset with someone, Dani realized. Working at night as she did, she was seldom able to enjoy this simple pleasure. Not that you'd call a sunset in this exotic place ordinary or simple—"magnificent," "awe-inspiring," "wondrous" were better descriptions of day's end in the South Pacific. But she had the feeling that, with Hamp, it wouldn't have mattered where they were. "I don't know what the others are like, but Huahine seems so—unspoiled," she murmured.

"The ambience here is probably closest to the Tahiti of the eighteenth century, but all the islands have been affected by civilization to some degree."

He touched the ends of her hair, only the ends, but Dani felt the electricity all the way to her scalp. "I read *Mutiny on the Bounty* in high school," she said hastily to hide her too-ready response.

"Some of the descendants of the crew moved to Tahiti from Pitcairn and still live in the islands." He continued the motion almost absently. "What an exciting discovery it must have been. Imagine, sailing across the world's biggest ocean on one of those old wooden schooners, day after day with the beams groaning and creaking to remind you of the instability of your craft, only water on the horizon. Suddenly a lookout spies land, land that wasn't on the charts. You'd have to find a break in the coral reef. As you skim over the water, closing in on the island, the mountains begin to take shape, then the trees—palms, banyan, chestnut—the luxurious vegetation, the flowers. The color of the water beneath your ship lightens gradually from deep almost blue-black, to royal blue, to the purest aquamarine."

Caught up in his scenario, she smiled at a private thought.

He dipped his chin to look at her face. "Why are you smiling?" he asked "Am I talking like the professor again?"

"Yes, but I like it." Dani let her head fall back to rest on the muscular arm behind her. The shadows had deepened with the setting of the sun, but her eyes had adjusted to the dim light. His intelligent brow, the solid jawline, were fully visible for her to study. "I was thinking not long ago that you had the soul of a pirate and the heart of a poet. Now I'll have to include dreamer in there somewhere."

"Dreamer?" Hamp touched her nose. He smiled, not displeased by the idea. "I suppose I am, in a way. Sandy would say 'workaholic,'" he inserted wryly. "But sometimes I think it would be exciting to have lived back then, to sail over a new horizon, one no one has ever sailed before."

"Tell me how you began," she urged softly, wanting him to go on, enjoying the sound of his deep voice.

"My grandfather. He was an amateur historian himself, and not a careless one. But he treated the subject like an avocation and expected the same of me." As he spoke, his voice became distracted. His gaze ran over Dani's oval face, beautiful in repose. Her eyes were closed; her lips were curved in a small half smile as she listened. Her hair flowed over his arm like a hot river of molten fire. The long elegant line of her throat was an alluring temptation to his lips. "He never understood why I couldn't give it part of my life and devote the remainder to the newspaper business."

Newspapers? A small frown appeared on Dani's brow. Lowell was a common name in California. There were Lowells all over the city of Palo Alto. Lowell lawyers and doctors, Lowell accountants. Surely there must be another Lowell newspaper besides the one— She opened her eyes.

Hamp's dark, sultry gaze was there waiting for hers, grabbing, holding, refusing to release her eyes. All other thoughts went out of her mind, all other feeling, clearing the way for pure sensation.

"I thought I had put you to sleep," he said huskily.

He knew better, but she started to shake her head, to tell him anyway. Suddenly the arm behind her tightened across her shoulders, lifting her toward him, suddenly his lips were on her throat, burning hot as he trailed moist, hungry kisses over her skin. He murmured her name, over and over. By the time his mouth reached her own she had lost her breath and gratefully took his into her mouth, her lungs.

His big hand settled on her breast, the thin silk of her blouse and the delicate lace of her bra no barrier to his probing fingers. "Ah, Dani. You fit my hand so well. I want to see you," he whispered between slow, hungry kisses. He loosened the buttons quickly and when her blouse was open to the waist he raised his head to look at her. Turned as she was in half profile, the mysterious shadows of the night added a seductive enticement to the curve of her breasts. "Beautiful," he whispered. "You're so beautiful. Are your breasts sensitive to a man's touch? Do you want my hands on you?"

Dani's nails dug into the muscles of his arm, but not in denial. "Yes." Oh, yes. Her need was quick; her desire instant. She wanted his hands, his mouth on her, all over her. Her blood sang through her veins. She had never felt this way before—so greedy, so avid, that she knew if he didn't fulfill his promise, if he didn't touch her soon, she'd die with the wanting. Desperately she inhaled.

"Slow, honey. Take it slow." A smile of pleasure at her response curved his firm mouth. He traced the flesh, now swelling over the tiny half-cups of her bra, to the hollow between her breasts with a teasing brush of his fingertips. He let the backs of his knuckles graze her nipple, but only lightly, still teasing. He could feel the hardness of the nub, straining against the lace.

"Hamp." It was a demand not a plea. Restlessly she moved against him. His hardness thrust against her hip, intensifying her need.

He freed her then, coaxing the delicate lace down.

Dani felt a wonderful relief as the lace was peeled away. It had become suddenly and unbearably abrasive.

Hamp closed his eyes for an instant, then opened them again. The material bunched underneath her breasts, tilting them up in bold invitation. Her nipples were erect in a pouty pose that was almost too much for his control. He growled, a soft but dangerous sound from deep within his chest. His mouth opened as he bent his head, his tongue darting out to taste her nipple before he closed over her and suckled hungrily. She tasted like heaven, like honey and nectar, like ambrosia for the gods.

Dani's fingers plunged into his hair, gripped to hold him close. The sharp pleasure went directly from his mouth through her body to excite the very core of her femininity. She felt his arousal, hard and insistent now, against her hip. "Oh, Hamp," she whispered, her voice husky and warm.

He raised his head to look deep into her eyes. The background noises—the tropical night—faded, leaving them encapsulated as though they had begun a journey in a bubble out of time and space, in a world of their own. His mouth returned to hers, his tongue exploring every velvet surface inside, every sharp, slick edge. His hand sought the warmth between her legs.

Low, intimate laughter, from a few steps away, brought them back to earth. Other couples were strolling about, others were drawn to the magic of the night.

Hamp wrenched his mouth away and buried his face in her hair, holding her tightly. Gradually the sound of their breathing diminished, the spiral slowed to a lazy spin.

With a last, long sigh, Dani shifted in his arms and began to button her blouse.

Hamp raised his head. He brushed her hair back from her face. "I've never wanted any woman the way I want you, Dani. Will you stay with me tonight?"

She lifted her hand to stroke the strong planes of his face. "I want to," she said honestly.

He searched her features, then he heaved a frustrated sigh. His big hands circled her waist and he gave her a boost. He retrieved their shoes and came up beside her. "But you won't," he said, drawing her under his arm.

She started to say something, but he stopped her with a short, hard kiss. "You don't have to explain. I know—the kids."

She took her shoes from him, carrying them by the narrow straps. "David is—we've sort of gotten in the habit of checking on each other. He would expect me to be listening for him to come in."

"Yeah, Sandy, too. And it's not the sort of habit you'd want them to break." Without further conversation they turned up the path that led toward their rooms. When they reached her door, he dropped his arm, but he wasn't ready to leave her.

She dug into her pocket for the key. When the door was open she turned back to him. A small light fixture over the door illuminated her face, the expression in her eyes an echo of his frustration. He held her gaze, plunging his free hand into his pocket, jingling the change there, to keep from grabbing her.

Lord, she was special—so very special.

"On the other hand..." she said, her smile soft and blurred at the edges.

He met the smile tenderly. "What?" he asked.

She reached out, tugging the hand out of his pocket, turning his wrist so she could read his watch. "It would be against all the laws of nature and the species for teenagers to go to bed before midnight." She paused. "You've left me with an unbearable ache, Hamp."

Hamp didn't bother to confirm the time. Before the sentence was complete he'd backed her into the room, slammed the door, and leaned against it, pulling her between his legs as his mouth sought hers in the dark.

Dani heard his shoes hit the floor and tossed hers in the same direction before she slid her arms around the strong column of his neck. The intervening minutes since they'd held each other on the beach might never have happened. Their passion returned like a surging wave, instantly, hungrily, drowning them in pure sensation. He held her tightly as he fumbled behind him for the safety lock.

The sound of its click in the silence of the room made her pause. It had been a very long time since she had known a man. To her surprise, she found herself feeling definitely uneasy, more than a bit timid.

Hamp felt the hesitation through her slender body. He touched the wall switch beside them, filling the room with a soft light from the beside lamp. He raised his head and put her slightly away from him. When she lifted her face he was met with an expression of almost predestined acceptance.

At the unexpected look, his breathing faltered imperceptibly. He struggled with his need until he had it fairly well under control. "We don't have to do this," he told her evenly.

She lifted her chin. "I want to."

"Dani," he murmured. A small smile hovered around his mouth as he raised his hand to her hair, stroking from the crown to her shoulder. His fingers closed over the slight bones there to draw her forward into his arms again. He settled her comfortably against him and rested his chin on her head. "Then why do you look like a maiden about to be sacrificed to the gods of the volcano?"

She tucked her face into his neck and her arms encircled his waist. Their legs brushed, setting off small explosions of desire within her. "I want to," she repeated. "But I haven't—it's been a long time—"

Her words were softly spoken, almost lost against the skin of his neck. He had to bend his head to hear. "Ah, honey." He wrapped his hand around the curve of her jaw, encouraging her to look at him again. "If that's the reason, I promise I'll take it very slow. You can stop me anytime you don't feel comfortable." His smile became wry. "Up to a certain point, that is."

She smiled, relaxing in his embrace. This was what she liked most about him: his ability to make the most unfamiliar situation seem perfectly natural. "And what happens at this certain point?"

"At that moment I turn into a crazed animal, a beast," he teased, grinning. His teeth were startlingly white against his tanned face.

"Crazed, huh?" Dani touched his lower lip with a finger and he gave her a demonstration, growling and nipping at her fingertip.

She laughed, her doubts forgotten. "Make love to me, Hamp," she whispered huskily.

His hand slid into her hair. "Are you sure?" he asked.

His expression was a study in control. If she hadn't felt the slight trembling in his fingertips, she would have thought him unmoved, so easy with his tone. She was safe with him. He would neither coerce her nor push her. And when this ended, there would be no strings. They had agreed.

"I'm sure," she said firmly. "I'm absolutely, completely, totally su—" she repeated in the instant before his lips covered hers.

He maneuvered her toward the bed, stopping on the way to remove her blouse, her bra. He undressed her slowly, relishing the revelation of each beautiful part of her body, touching her, murmuring praise, and wiping away any remaining traces of shyness. Sitting on the edge of the mattress, she helped him out of his clothes, too, but he was less patient with the confining barriers of his own and so was she. Her blood was racing madly through her veins. "Hamp," she whispered as she stroked the thatch of hair that covered his broad chest. It felt wiry, exciting under her fingers.

He was beautifully made, wide shouldered, narrow hipped. His body was not that of a young man, but bore a stamp of experience, of nobility and pure masculinity that was so much more electrifying to her than youth would have been.

He tipped her back onto the bed and covered her body with his, pressing her gently into the comforter. His name was a whisper on her lips, a gasp of inflamed arousal when he entered her. Their eyes met. Breathing heavily, his muscles shaking with the effort, he allowed her time to accept him, time to grow used to the feeling of a man inside her. Then he began to move and the flames within her grew in intensity, engulfing them both, setting off simultaneous shudders of rapture as they clung to each other.

Neither of them had to ask if the other had been moved by the experience. Hamp turned to his side, keeping her in the circle of his arms. This was the perfect place to be, thought Dani drowsily, feeling warm and blissful and extravagantly satiated. If heaven were on earth, this would be it.

Dani had no idea how much time had passed, minutes or hours, while he stroked the skin of her back, let his fingers comb softly through her hair, touched her lips, her cheek, her brow, gently, with his lips. Not a kiss really, more like an affectionate greeting.

At last he sighed and so did she. Keeping her in the curve of his arm he twisted to glance at the watch he'd tossed onto the bedside table. "It's eleven-thirty." He cupped her face in his large hand, tilting her head back. "I suppose I'd better go," he said, his expression serious.

Her head was resting on his arm. When she nodded she felt the contraction of muscle there. "I suppose so," she said, allowing him to read her regret.

"I have a couple of interviews in the morning, but I thought I'd see if I can find a sailboat for us tomorrow afternoon. Would you like to go out?"

She smiled and said softly, "I'd love it. I haven't been sailing in years."

Something else Davey had probably taught her, thought Hamp, but he didn't ask. He didn't trust himself to kiss her again, so he released her and stood, reaching for his clothes.

Dani was right behind him. She pulled on her shirt and slacks. When he turned to lift a brow in inquiry, she smiled a bit self-consciously. "If the children see you coming out of my room . . ." She left the rest unsaid as she kicked her underthings under a chair.

Hamp felt annoyed, and at the same time guilty for feeling that way. "Should we make up the bed, too?"

She shot him a look. "We didn't unmake it."

Now he was embarrassed. "Damn." He went to her and pulled her into his arms. "I'm sorry, Dani. It's just that I don't like having to hop out of bed and cover up—pretend nothing ever happened. And I don't want to leave you."

Dani wound her arms around him and lay her head on his chest. "I understand. I don't want you to leave."

His arms tightened. "What can we do about it?"

"We can sit outside and look at the sky and talk," she suggested, leaning back in his arms to see how he felt about the suggestion. He grinned.

"What are your plans when David's out of college?" he asked when they were settled on the sweet-smelling grass outside the cabin.

The music of her laughter fell lightly on the evening air. "That's at least four years away," she protested. "I tend to live one year at a time."

He looked down at this woman he'd just made love to with a depth of emotion he hadn't felt in years, if ever. The moonlight defined her features with silver, illuminating her swollen lips, her mussed hair. If the kids came along now they would have no doubt as to what their parents had been doing. He hid a smile and dragged his gaze away from her unbound breasts beneath the silky fabric.

She had begun with so little and accomplished so much. And in the struggle, she'd lost not one whit of her femininity or the passion that made her so womanly.

Having the sole responsibility for a young son when she was so young herself would have weighed heavily on those slender shoulders. There must have been occasions when she was younger, when she had wished for freedom. He didn't doubt her love for David, but she must have longed for her youth to be returned to her. "Surely you must have thought about it?"

"Yes," Dani said slowly. She curled her long legs under her sideways, sitting on one hip and balancing her body, straight-armed. "I have thought about it a lot. I've always wanted to go back to school." She paused, uncertain, and plucked at a blade of grass. Hamp had shared his dreams with her. Could she reciprocate? She'd never talked about this to anyone else, not even to David. "Once I even enrolled," she finally admitted.

"You did?"

"David was six, he'd begun the first grade."

"I know a number of women who've gone back after their children started school." He waited, knowing there was more. Something had very obviously thwarted her ambition. "What happened?" he finally asked.

"Appendicitis happened," she answered on a long sigh. "Not me. David. And no insurance is what happened. Please don't mention this in front of him. He'd likely drop out of school so I could go."

"I won't mention it," he assured her. "What did you want to study?"

"Everything," she said immediately. She shot him a glance from beneath her lowered lashes. "You won't laugh?"

His smile was puzzled. "Why would I laugh?"

"I want to study art," she admitted. "Oh, not 'how to,' but art appreciation. I want to see the great paintings and sculptures of the world and I want to understand them when I see them."

"What's wrong with that?" He was still puzzled by her diffident attitude.

"It's impractical, that's what." Dani shifted restlessly. It was time to end this conversation. She had already revealed too much. "If I ever do get to go to school I should study business," she said brusquely. "I should learn how to keep my own books and figure my own taxes, so I wouldn't have to pay so much to have it done for me."

When she would have risen, Hamp caught her arm and held her. "You should do exactly what you want to do. And if you want, you can have both."

"That sounds good in theory, Hamp; but real life doesn't work that way. Not for regular people."

The fingers on her arm tightened; he leaned closer. "'Regular people'? As opposed to what other kind?"

She waved a hand. "Your life-style . . ." Her voice trailed off.

"What the hell are you talking about? Who do you think I am?"

"You are a man who flies first-class and takes limos." She touched his cheek, smiling to take the sting out of her words. "I don't mean that unkindly, but you are one of the newspaper Lowells, aren't you?" When he nodded, she gently released herself from his grip and went on in a lighter tone, which she hoped didn't betray her sudden need to escape. "For the rest of us there are always bills larger than you can pay. Just when you think everything is going well, something happens to put you two steps behind where you started. You're better-off not expecting too much." She rose and this time he didn't stop her. "I'm tired. Good night, Hamp."

She was inside before Hamp could think of an answer for her, leaving him sitting alone and a bit dumbfounded. He knew she'd had a difficult time. Didn't she realize how much he admired her for her accomplishments?

Dani shut the door behind her and leaned against the wood. So, he *was* a member of that branch of the Lowell family, the richest and most powerful of them all. It was another barrier between them.

Two years ago this summer, boosted by the backing of Lawrence Lowell and the Lowell newspapers, the county sheriff had begun an investigation into the criminal connections of certain local nightclubs. At the end of the investigation, Foxy's had been completely vindicated and that fact had been published clearly—probably to insure against a lawsuit. Lawrence had even called her once to congratulate her on the vindication. She'd taken great pleasure in hanging up on him. But the club, and Dani, had felt the ill effects of the whole predicament for several months. Traces of her bitterness would probably always remain.

She'd thought about telling Hamp about what had happened. But he'd forsworn the newspaper business for teaching. He couldn't be blamed for the behavior of his family.

Hamp was different, she told herself, but still she needed some time alone to adjust to this new knowledge.

DANI KNEW IMMEDIATELY that something was very wrong when she met the others for lunch the next day. Sandy was subdued and, if the muscle in his jaw was any indication, Hamp was furious. David seemed to be staying out of it. They had gone into the village this morning for Hamp to meet with some of the leaders there.

She wondered what had happened, but refrained from asking. Instead she went about trying to restore harmony with quiet conversation.

When lunch was over, David and Sandy returned to the rooms for the scuba-diving equipment while Hamp and Dani lingered over coffee.

"Is it anything I can help with?" she asked Hamp.

He ran a frustrated hand through his hair. "Hell, I don't know."

"It can't be all that bad."

"Don't defend her," he warned, his dark brows meeting. "Her flippant attitude nearly caused me to lose one of my most important contacts here, Dani. I didn't hear the exact words myself but she evidently made a smart remark to one of the village leaders this morning about trading beads with the natives. The man was highly offended, as you can imagine. Thank God, he has grandchildren of his own. He gave her a quick and effective put-down and called her a child. That shut her up for the rest of the morning. Dammit, Dani. Doesn't she have any feelings for other people?"

Dani was surprised by his description of the incident, but she couldn't answer his question. She needed time to digest the information. Such thoughtlessness and inconsiderate behavior didn't sound like the Sandy she was beginning to know. Hamp seemed surprised, too. "Did you try to talk to her about what happened?"

"No. I was so mad I couldn't say a word. I might have ended up shouting at her."

"Maybe that was what she wanted."

He opened his mouth to say something else, but just then David and Sandy returned and the opportunity was lost. "The boat's here," David told him.

The sea outside the lagoon was rough. Dani reveled in its turbulence. Old skills came back to her as Hamp barked out orders. Sandy was a competent sailor, and David—well, David was a fast learner.

Dani watched her son fondly. He was enjoying this every bit as much as his father would have. She wished there had been more time to make sure he was exposed to things like sailing. But there had never been enough. Time was the enemy, had always been the enemy, and now that he was about to enter college, she was very close to losing her child to adulthood.

The realization was both depressing and comforting. Depressing because they had been so close; comforting because David was going to be a fine man.

"Heads up!" shouted Hamp, recalling Dani to herself. She narrowly missed being dumped into the sea.

She smiled unrepentantly. "Sorry, captain."

Keeping one hand firmly on the tiller, Hamp held out his arm. "Leave the line to Sandy and come here," he ordered sternly.

Sparing only a brief thought for the children, she obeyed, picking her way carefully aft over the slick deck to sit beside him. After the kiss Sandy and David had witnessed yesterday there wasn't much point in avoiding him.

Hamp liked the feeling of her there, liked her body nestled warmly next to his, liked the way her arm slid naturally around his waist.

Dani sighed, secure in the comfortable feeling of his support on the rocking boat, the warmth that radiated from his body.

"You're a pretty good sailor," he observed, keeping his eyes on a spot of water just beyond the bow.

"Davey—"

"I know. Davey taught you," he said with a crooked smile. "Davey must have been quite a man."

"Davey was a bit of a pirate, too," she told him with a grin.

It was stupid as hell to be jealous of a dead man. "There's a deserted beach with an interesting coral formation just beyond that headland. I thought we'd anchor for a while and do some diving."

"Sounds good."

The tiny cove was shaped like a half-moon, its white beach fringed with palms. There wasn't a vestige of civilization in sight. When the boat was secure Dani dug into her bag for her sunscreen. "Would you like for me to do your back?" said a voice from behind her.

"Please," Dani answered as she shucked her shorts. "Be glad you aren't a redhead, Sandy."

"You have a nice tan now."

Dani smiled at the unhappy young girl. "Meaning I looked like something out of a Dracula movie when we arrived."

Sandy smiled, too, but it was a halfhearted attempt. She looked around before she spoke again. Hamp and David were already over the side and swimming, facedown, in a line parallel to the shore. "Dani, could I talk to you?"

"Sure, honey. What's on your mind?" Dani said carefully.

"Daddy and I had a terrible argument this morning."

Dani was quiet for a minute, wondering if she should reveal her knowledge of the incident. "I know," she finally conceded softly.

"You mean he *told* you about it? Everything?" Sandy was stiff in her outrage. "How *could* he?"

Dani dismissed her indignant affront for what it was, the normal teenage tendency to overdramatize and distract attention from the true problem. "It was pretty obvious at lunch that something was wrong. I asked him if I could help."

The young girl slumped on the seat, the diving mask dangling from one hand. "He's really disappointed in me."

"Well." She needed to be careful here. "You didn't exactly use the greatest tact. The man in the village . . ."

"I know. Sometimes I open my big mouth . . . and I'm always sorry. But I don't mean just this morning. I mean, he's disappointed in me in general."

"Oh, Sandy, that isn't true. Your daddy loves you very much."

"I know that, too. And I love him. I'd love to be what he wants me to be, but I'm not. He hates my boyfriend. Rocky may not be Hampton Lowell's idea of a perfect gentleman, but he's fun. He doesn't make me feel like a dummy. I'll never be smart like Daddy is. I mean, my grades are okay, but I'm not a genius like David. And I know I worry him, but he just doesn't understand."

Uh-oh. She'd heard that refrain, too. "Honey..."

The face turned to her was a feminine version of her father's, and so hopeful. The blue eyes alone were a sure legacy from her mother. If only I could straighten out the world for you, thought Dani. She decided to be honest. "Honey," she repeated. "Your daddy wants you to be yourself. He worries about you just as I worry about David. It's in the nature of parents to worry. And sometimes not to understand."

"Why would you worry about David? He's perfect." The sarcasm there was plain, and the hint of jealousy, too.

"I used to worry about his not being able to ease up on himself. I was afraid for a while that if he didn't learn, he'd grow into an inflexible man."

"Like Daddy," Sandy pronounced flatly, looking out over the water where the men were swimming. Her blue eyes were bleak. "He thinks I'm a child."

"Your behavior this morning was pretty childish, wasn't it? Your father is trying, Sandy. Believe me, he's trying." She put all the sincerity she was feeling into her voice.

"Would you talk to him, Dani? Please?"

"Sandy, I don't think—"

Sandy broke in. "Please, Dani. Please, please, please. He thinks I'm just a kid. He'd listen to you if you tried to make him understand about women."

Dani hid her amusement. She didn't think it would be wise to interfere, but she could drop a few hints. What could that hurt? "Well," she drawled the word tentatively.

"Oh, thank you, Dani."

Suddenly David's head broke the surface of the water. He pushed back his mask and lifted an arm to wave toward the boat. "Hey, Dandy Sandy!" he shouted. "Come on in. The water's great!"

"Dandy Sandy?"

Sandy blushed slightly and handed back the tube of sunscreen. "Yeah, isn't that a dumb name?" But Dani could see that she was pleased. *Bless you for your insight, David. Why did I ever worry about you?*

Sandy adjusted her mask and dived in. The sunscreen was dropped forgotten on the seat as Dani followed.

"Oh-h-h," moaned Dani as she reached for the phone. "Hello?"

"Mom, where are you?"

"David," she said patiently. "I'm in the room that has the telephone that you dialed."

"I mean where *are* you? We're ready to eat and there's a show—a group from Samoa—that's going to start in fifteen minutes."

"Honey, I'm not hungry right now. I'll order from room service later."

"Mom, you know you have to be careful. Why didn't you use your sunscreen?"

"Hey, will you get off my back, please?" Just the thought sent a painful shudder through her. "Besides, I forgot. You enjoy the show and I'll see you in the morning."

Dani wasn't really surprised when the knock sounded on her door soon after she hung up. And she wasn't surprised to find Hamp there instead of her son. "Oh-h-h," she moaned again as she staggered to her feet. "Wait a minute," she called. She wrapped her robe around her sideways, trying to cover the strategic spots while avoiding the tender places on her body, which were almost everywhere. She opened the door a crack and peered around the edge. "Go away."

"I've brought something that will help." He had a tray in his hands. A plate of fresh fruit and a glass of juice and something else in a bottle, which she couldn't identify.

"An old island cure, huh? Are you going to rub me with papaya?" But she eyed the glass of juice thirstily.

"An old island cure called witch hazel."

She wrinkled her nose—even that hurt. "No, thank you. I've already put something on it. And I took two aspirin. Now, leave me to suffer until it goes away."

Hamp observed that pain had dulled those vivid light green eyes to a greenish-gray. "Let me in, Dani. The witch hazel will cool your skin and you need to drink something so you won't get dehydrated."

"I'll take the juice." She reached a bare arm around the door and took the frosty glass from the tray. "But you can't come in. I'm not trying to be provocative when I say this— in fact it's the last thing on my mind right now—but I don't have any clothes on."

He laughed, but the picture conjured up by her words wasn't funny. "Okay, close the door and go jump under the covers."

She had put her lips to the rim of the glass, but at his words, she grimaced. "The covers! Are you insane? Those sheets are starched!"

"Hmm." Hamp thought a minute. He watched her swollen eyelids drift shut as she gulped the cold juice. His heart went out to her. "Honey, go get your *pareu*," he said compassionately.

She opened her eyes. "Why?"

When she licked the juice off her upper lip, Hamp almost dropped the tray. "Remember how soft the material is?" he encouraged. "Just wrap it around you. The witch hazel will feel good, I promise."

Dani hesitated. She really needed to talk to him about the conversation she'd had with Sandy this afternoon. In a roundabout way that conversation was the reason for this whole fiasco. She *never* forgot her sunscreen. Unless she was distracted by an important matter.

"Okay," she relented. She returned the glass to his tray, shut the door in his face and went to the drawer. The *pareu* was soft, much softer than terry cloth, much softer than starched sheets. Gingerly she tied the fabric in a loose knot above her breasts, checked to make sure she was decent and called for Hamp to come in.

The next few minutes were to be endured, not enjoyed, thought Hamp, as he entered the room. Clearly she was in no mood for seduction. She was perched on the very edge of the only straight chair in the room. Her wet bathing suit lay where it had been dropped, a terry-cloth robe was on the floor by the door, a wet towel graced the threshold of the bathroom. The other clothes she'd worn today were in a bundle in the middle of the dresser.

"Poor Dani," he murmured as he scooted the bundle aside to make room for the tray. Lowering his glasses to the end of his nose, he settled his hands on his hips and surveyed her over the rims. Her hair drooped, her shoulders drooped, the corners of her mouth drooped. "You are the most pitiful sight I've ever seen," he said gently. "Do you know how much I want to pick you up and comfort you?"

"Don't you dare," she said quickly, but she smiled, touched by his concern. "But thanks for the thought."

"Maybe another time. Now we've got to do something to make you feel better." He pushed his glasses back into place and grinned. "While we protect your modesty. Didn't you buy several *pareus*?"

"Yes, but I don't want to get witch hazel on them, Hamp."

"It won't stain and the smell will wash out," he assured her. "I think this will work best if you lie on one and put the other one over you."

Grumbling all the time, she finally managed to get herself arranged to his satisfaction. It didn't hurt nearly as much when she lay on her stomach, she discovered. Her back was burned more severely.

Hamp bit back a curse as he pulled the material down until it just covered her hips. This had to hurt like hell, but except for a few incoherent mumblings, she hadn't complained this afternoon. "Dani, this looks pretty bad. Do you think we should call a doctor?" he asked quietly.

She shook her head; resting her forehead on her folded arms she said, "No, believe me, it looks worse than it is. I'll be much better tomorrow. My skin is so fair that the red shows more than on a brunette."

His gaze was drawn to her side, to the rounded curve of her breast. Fair. Yes, it was fair where the sun had not reached. As fair as new snow, as fair as a baby's skin. And as smooth as satin, he knew.

He took a deep breath and went to work, glad that he had brought plenty of cotton. He soaked a large square, making a compress to place on one shoulder.

Dani caught her breath as the cold compress hit her hot skin.

"Does that hurt?"

"No," she assured him when she could speak again. "The cold was a shock, that's all. It feels wonderful."

For a long time he continued alternating the compresses until, finally, he saw her eyelids drift shut. "Go to sleep if you can. I'll lock the door on my way out."

Dani turned her head far enough to give him a sleepy smile. "Thank you, Hamp. I feel so much better." She'd forgotten that she'd planned to talk to him about Sandy.

For a long time Hamp stood by the bed, looking down at the still, sleeping woman, thinking. He took no pleasure in having Dani vulnerable. It prompted an unfamiliar fear—a fear of deepening emotional involvement, a fear of tenderness and caring too much. With a great deal of effort he forced those fears from the forefront of his mind, where they interfered with rational thinking, to a spot near the back, where he could examine the reason for them with more objectivity.

He'd been fooling himself. From the first moment he'd glimpsed her in the airport, he'd been intrigued by her. She was unique. Where she was concerned, his emotions were not so easily controlled as they were with other women. The week in Tahiti would soon be over. In a couple of days they would be leaving for home. Things—things like feelings and emotions—might change when they got back to California, but he didn't think so. Not since the chaos that was his adolescence had he felt this wonderful, paralyzing sweetness.

The question that was skirting the edge of his thoughts, nudging him persistently, finally insisted on acknowledgement. Was he falling in love with Dani Fox?

He could be, he finally admitted; he very well could be. And that would present him with a whole new set of problems. He would have to make a choice. Did he want his life to continue as it was, safe and contained, or did he want to try for life as it might be? And what kind of cooperation would he get from the independent woman on the bed?

After a while he began to pick up the clothing that was strewn all over the room, hanging the wet towel and bathing suit over the shower rod in the bathroom, folding the rest. Then he turned out the light and locked the door as he left.

7

By the time Dani rejoined the group she recognized the hiatus as a blessing. It had given her time to reestablish her emotional guard.

She had lost nearly two days of her vacation for her carelessness. David had told her, when she asked, that Hamp and Sandy were treating each other with wary courtesy. He, David, often found himself in the middle, but surprisingly he didn't grumble about it.

Hamp stayed in touch by telephone. He included David in his plans for himself and Sandy, but he didn't come back to her room. When she wasn't sleeping off the effects of the tropical sun, she realized she missed him. And she didn't like the hollowness that accompanied that sentiment.

Hamp was easy to talk to; she'd told him things about her feelings and her dreams that she'd never admitted to another person. These two days away from him was a godsend, she told herself. They gave her time to step back and evaluate the situation. She could enjoy his company as long as she recognized the threat that he represented to her peace of mind and independence.

He was the sort of man who would dominate—quietly but thoroughly. He would want an ordered life, his meals on time.

She must be amiable, but she repeated her admonition to herself to hold some of her feelings in reserve, just in case.

Hamp smiled across the breakfast table at the fully re-covered Dani. "I think we should celebrate your return to the land of the living," he said with a smile.

"Celebrate? How?" she asked, pleased at the suggestion.

"We could rent an outrigger this time, go back to the cove and have a cookout."

"What would we cook?" said Sandy, frowning.

"We could fish, I suppose," offered David without much more enthusiasm than Sandy was showing. "But I'm not much of a fisherman."

"Good. And since we're in Polynesia," said Dani, "we'll have a luau and cook a pig, or part of one." She patted her son's hand. "To be on the safe side."

"Not a luau, Mom. The Tahitian language has no *L*."

"That's right," she remembered. "Okay, we'll have a feast—a *tama'ara'a.*"

David's eyes widened in surprise. "Well, well. I'm im-pressed."

"You should be," she told him with a grin. She'd bought a language phrase book in Papeete. "Actually, I haven't had much to do except read for the past two days."

Hamp watched the byplay between mother and son, but the cookout idea was not prevalent in his thoughts. Dani was. He didn't want to disrupt the holiday mood—the three of them were caught up in their plans—so he simply ob-served. She was dressed this morning in a short, bright, lemon-yellow one-piece thing—a sort of a romper—with no sleeves, buttons down the front and an elastic waist. He couldn't help thinking how convenient those buttons would be, if they were alone.

He'd known the night he'd nursed her burns that he had come awfully close to saying things he hadn't thought through completely. Now, two days later, he still hadn't thought them through. His mind was having a war with his heart and he cautioned himself to withhold some of his feelings, just in case.

After breakfast they separated, each to be responsible for part of the preparations. Hamp had a meeting with the team of British anthropologists who were recording the music of the islands that day, but he promised to see to the fire and the fishing gear. And he would cook.

David was dispatched to find and rent an outrigger canoe. Dani questioned the wisdom of trying to paddle a canoe, even one with the built-in stability of an outrigger and even in the relatively calm waters of the lagoon. She was informed by her son that most of the craft were motorized today.

Sandy was in charge of decorations and mundane things like forks and plates. She protested that the ancient Polynesians didn't have forks and plates, but she was overruled.

Dani hitched a ride to the village in the hotel Jeep to shop for groceries.

THE FEAST on the beach of the secluded cove was a perfect end to a hectic day of preparation. They had eaten until they were stuffed. The remains of roast pork, breadfruit, melon, yams, and, surprisingly an *ava*, a gray salmon that David had caught, were repacked in baskets and ready to be loaded into the canoe. When they left there would be no sign that they had ever been here except for their footprints in the sand. And those would be wiped away by the next tide. Torches, scavenged from the hotel supply, were beginning to throw deep shadows on the sand; soon it would be very dark.

David and Sandy wandered to a point of the cove, a hundred yards away. As she and Hamp lounged comfortably on woven grass mats watching the last of the daylight disappear, Dani considered something she would like to have forgotten: her promise to Sandy to talk to her father.

Hamp had been in a pleasant mood all evening. By unspoken agreement the argument with his daughter seemed to have been tabled—not forgotten, but set aside. Dani was reluctant to put an end to their truce.

However, Sandy had reminded her of her promise a few hours ago.

She looked over at him. With the loss of sunlight the air was cooler, as he had warned them it would be. He'd put on a light-weight sweat suit over his swimming trunks. His strong build wasn't disguised at all by the baggy cut. He was stretched out, his torso propped on his elbows, his legs crossed at the ankles. There were wet spots where the material clung, at the tops of his thighs, over his prominent sex.

Wrenching her attention from his strong sensual appeal, Dani jumped up. Busily, she found her jeans and a long-sleeved shirt to pull over her romper. When she was dressed she sat down again on the mat facing him and crossed her legs, Indian style. "Hamp, may I talk to you about Sandy?" she said.

He rolled to his side, cradled his cheek on one hand and looked at her with a small smile on his lips. "I don't think that's a good idea." He stretched his arm over the space between them to lay a hand on her thigh. "Surely we can find better things to talk about," he said in a husky voice, while his thumb traced the inseam of her jeans.

Why did his touch leave her feeling like jelly inside? It took all her effort to fight against the fire that ignited under his fingers. "Please, Hamp."

Brown eyes tangled with green. "I didn't ask for this, Dani," he warned. "I don't want to argue with you."

"I don't want to argue, either, and if you get mad at me, you'll be justified. But Sandy did ask. I want you to know that. Otherwise I'd mind my own business."

He withdrew his hand and made a noise that she considered for a minute before she decided it was an affirmative. A grudging affirmative, but an affirmative nevertheless. She tossed her hair over her shoulder and folded her hands together in her lap.

Hamp watched Dani's hands. They were too still. That she didn't relish what she was about to do was obvious. He felt a flare of irritation at his daughter for bringing Dani into their quarrel. "She can talk to me," he said, hating the defensive tone he heard in his own voice. Abruptly he sat up. Wrapping his arms around his knees, he stared out over the calm water. "I've never refused to listen to her."

"Let me see if I can put it to you like she put it to me. She said, 'I know Daddy loves me, but I'm a disappointment to him because I'm not smart like he and David are.'"

Hamp turned his head to look at her, a frown between his brows. "She's jealous of David? Is that why she's wearing her martyred look these days?" His words came out on a snarl.

Dani couldn't believe what she was hearing. She knew firsthand how Hamp tried to be patient with Sandy. He would rather retreat than confront the child directly, and that wasn't always the wisest course. Surely this time, he hadn't . . . "I suppose you *told* her she was acting like a martyr."

His slight flush was answer enough to her accusation. She took a deep breath to control her temper. "Hamp, that's a personal criticism. Anyone would react that way. Don't you know that you can criticize someone's actions, but not what they are? You can tell her that she's behaved horribly. But don't say she's a horrible person." She used her hand to punctuate her words, then let it fall to her thigh where she rubbed against the denim agitatedly.

Because he knew the truth of her statement, Hamp was angry at her and at himself. He ground his back teeth together and stared out over the water for a minute before he answered. "I've never asked her to be anything except what she is," he bit out. "If she's told you differently, she's lying."

Oh, Lord, she was making it worse. "Hamp, Sandy isn't jealous of David himself, she's jealous of what the two of you share. The flippancy you hate so, the boyfriend with the earring, the punky haircut, the incident in the village—have you ever thought those things might be bids for attention? You're very occupied in your work."

"And when did you get your degree in psychology, Dr. Fox?" he asked sarcastically. He knew as soon as the words were out that the thrust had hit home. He could have hardly chosen a more effective way to wound than with the one subject she was sensitive about—her lack of schooling. She had shared that feeling of inadequacy in an intimate moment. He'd always despised people who used such personal revelations as weapons later. But dammit, he was hurt, too, by her quick and ready criticism. And sorry that he hadn't seen Sandy's motives for himself. "Dani—"

She recovered quickly. "Point to you, Professor. Maybe I don't have a high falutin' degree like you do, but I'll wager on myself over you any day when it comes to getting along with my child," she told him coolly. "Once you admitted that you had trouble understanding teenagers. I thought you were trying to come to terms with that, but it seems I was mistaken."

She rose in a fluid movement and bent to pick up the mat she'd been sitting on. With her other hand she let forth the shrill whistle Hamp was beginning to hate. Her face was a study in indifference. He knew, however, that her emotions were churning, as his were, under the surface composure. She rolled the mat, tucked it under her arm and picked up the basket.

He got to his feet, caught her arm and took the basket. "We seem to have a knack for striking out at the most sensitive spots, don't we?"

She sighed, nodding, and let the mat fall back to the ground.

"Did you and Davey fight a lot?" he asked, almost idly.

"All the time," she responded, recalling that Davey had always blamed her red hair. "I shouldn't have presumed to advise you on your relationship with your daughter. I'm sorry, Hamp."

"But she asked you to. She probably had to talk you into it. I don't imagine you agreed willingly."

His insight surprised her into a small smile. "No," she admitted. "I didn't want to interfere."

Hamp was encouraged by the smile, but he had to say it all. "And you were trying to help. I shouldn't have reacted so defensively. I should never have used things you told me in confidence as a way to get back at you, Dani. I can't imagine why I did," he said quietly. "Except that powerful emotions have to find release somehow." His voice was tight and raw.

Dani's eyes met his in surprise. "What . . ." But the kids came back on the run and the moment for explanations was lost.

IMPATIENT TO FINISH the discussion they'd almost had last night, Hamp was up early, prowling the grounds of the hotel, beginning to wonder if he'd missed Dani at breakfast. He looked at his watch. Nine-thirty. He had a stray thought for the youngsters. Sandy must be sleeping in this morning.

He was headed down the path toward her room when the door opened and Dani stood there, blinking against the bright sunlight. He paused to look at her, his mouth curved into an appreciative smile. She was obviously on her way to the beach. She was wearing the white bathing suit and sheer cover-up she'd worn that first morning at Maeva Beach. Today she'd added a huge floppy hat that shadowed her features beguilingly. He quickened his steps, gathering the thoughts that seemed to have fled at the sight of her.

Dani didn't notice the man on the path. Her attention had been distracted by something on the floor at her feet. She bent over to pick up a folded paper, recognizing it as a sheet of hotel stationery. She had read the few scrawled lines before she realized that she wasn't alone. She looked up to meet Hamp's steady gaze. "Good morning. You look very serious this morning."

"Good morning," he said. "I am serious." He caught her face between his hands and kissed her, very gently, very tenderly. She tasted of toothpaste. "I came to ask you to spend today with me. Alone. I'll find something to occupy the kids."

From under the rim of the hat her beautiful green eyes searched his. Finally she spoke: "They've taken care of that themselves, it seems." She held out the paper.

"'Mom'," he read. "'Sandy and I are going to the dig site near the *marae*. Afterward she wants to see the vanilla fields. We'll be back late this afternoon. Get Hamp to take you to a *motu*. You'll enjoy it, I'm sure, and the outrigger's paid for until four o'clock. Don't worry about us. Love, David.'"

Hamp must have read the note three times. At last he lifted his gaze, looked at her, his dark eyes were blacker than

Dani had ever seen them. "It sounds like a good idea to me. Do you want to?" he asked in a low voice.

Without the least doubt, Dani knew what he was really asking. Her heart began to pound, restlessly, rapidly. Even when they argued, the memory of their lovemaking had plagued her with a desire to repeat the experience. Her lashes dropped to shield her expression from him. An uninhabited spit of land. The two of them alone for the whole day under the palms.

"We could get the hotel to pack a lunch while you have breakfast," Hamp proposed. He wasn't going to push Dani, but, Lord, he wanted her alone out there. He wanted the disagreements forgotten, the promises fulfilled again.

"I have a better idea," she said at last, smiling up at him with a serenity that caused his pulse to race. "Let's have the hotel pack breakfast instead and go right now."

A *MOTU* is an atoll formed on the top of a coral reef, not born of volcanic activity. As such it is flat and subject to flooding during the storm season. All but the largest of them— the ones that have collected silt and sand from the ocean for centuries—are uninhabitable. The one Hamp took her to was relatively new, he explained, probably less than a hundred years old. It was not more than five hundred yards long and the width of a football field at its widest point. Thick stands of coconut palms grew to startling heights, shading most of the fragile patch of land.

As Hamp nosed the canoe toward the wide beach and cut the motor, Dani hopped out into water up to her thighs and helped guide it onto the sand, free of the sweep of the tides. He joined her with the picnic basket and a blanket. "Did you bring plenty of sunscreen today, or shall we stay under the trees?"

She looked around at the coconuts strewn over the ground and up at the trees, heavy with the fruit that grew in clusters just under their fronds. "I brought a whole tube. It looks risky under there."

He smiled and dropped the basket and blanket under a nearby tree. "Look again."

She placed her hand in his outstretched one. To her the area under the palms still looked dangerous and she told him so, even as she followed him into the shade.

"The fruit is green," he explained. "It doesn't drop until it turns brown. Come here, let me show you something else." He pulled her forward, pointing out the broken fruit where it had fallen. Little shoots had already begun to develop into little trees.

"If they sprout that quickly, why isn't the place like a jungle?"

"The shoots don't have a long life. Storms get most of them, and islanders gather some to replant on the mainland. Why don't you wander around? I'll finish unloading the canoe."

Dani watched him for as long as she dared, his muscular body bare except for his brief swimming trunks. His tanned back gleamed in the pattern of sun to shade as he worked. He was a beautifully made man, all muscle and sinew.

She knew he was as nervous as she, trying to present a sense of normality—friends out for the day—and she liked him for it. But she also knew that the eagerness was in him, too, and the desire. Postponement just scraped against her nerves, making her jumpy.

She turned toward the ocean side of the island. When she reached the beach she discovered that there wasn't much beach there. The waves pounding against the shelf of the reef kept the sand to a minimum width. She unbuttoned her white man-tailored cover-up, now damp along the tails.

Hooking it over one shoulder, she stood, staring at the horizon, understanding what Hamp meant when he said he felt like the only person in the world when he camped out here. But she wasn't. On the other side of this fragile spit of land was the other one.

She didn't hear his footsteps, and suddenly he was beside her. She turned toward him, slowly and deliberately.

"Dani," he murmured, stepping closer. "I've missed what I never knew before you."

She took a step, too, and they were only inches apart. She raised one hand to his chest and felt the shudder that ripped through him at her touch. His mouth came crashing down. Her lips were waiting, parted and moist. He released her mouth only long enough to whip off his glasses and toss them aside. They made no noise when they landed on the sand.

For Dani the excitement of the kiss, the anticipation of the lovemaking, was intensified by the understanding that their time in paradise was coming to a close. Nothing further could come of it. Tomorrow night they would leave Tahiti. Their loving would be only a memory, and she found her response was all the more heated for her awareness of its transience.

The white cover-up drifted, unnoticed to the sand. Her hands roamed restlessly over his back as she arched toward his body, wanting to be closer, and closer still. She gripped his broad shoulders, her nails digging into his sun-warmed skin.

Here in this wild, primitive place they kissed with wild, primitive abandon. Hamp took large mock bites of her mouth, while one big hand flattened her hips, crushing her to him. Dani rose on tiptoe, shifting her legs to fit her curves to the hard planes of his chest, his hips, his thighs.

His tongue thrust into the warm, sweet cavern of her mouth, sweeping, tasting with a hunger he wouldn't have believed even that night on the beach, a hunger unleashed by his knowledge of his own feelings. His fingers tangled in her hair, directing the angle of her head for his kiss. Her lips were moist and wonderful; he couldn't get enough of the taste of them. He ran his hands over her back and around to her breasts, bound lightly by the white one-piece bathing suit; he couldn't get enough of the feel of her body. Breaking off the kiss he stepped back to pull the suit down. She started to help.

"Let me," he said in a thick, rough tone. "It's something I've dreamed of doing since that first morning by the pool." As he slowly peeled the suit down, revealing first her breasts, then her tiny midriff, her flat, smooth stomach, he stopped to touch her lightly with wonder, as though he'd never touched her before. His breathing became almost desperately shallow. When he pulled the suit down over her hips, unveiling the soft thatch that was the guardian of her femininity, he wasn't breathing at all.

And Dani couldn't stand. He put his lips to the inside of her thigh. Her knees started to give. With a laugh that was purely male, Hamp swept her up into his arms, intending to return to the other side of the island, to the blanket. But with his first step he faltered, still holding her firmly to his chest, and looked down at her love-drugged features. "I don't have my glasses on and that blanket is a hell of a long way away." His voice was the voice of a man whose blood ran hot and hungry.

"Too far," she concurred.

Carefully he laid her on the warm sand. He shed his suit in one motion and loomed large over her, reminding Dani suddenly of the animal he'd called himself. But not the beast; never that. He was beautiful, like an eagle, strong and soaring; or a big jungle cat, his grace and bold sinew inherent; or a stag, proud and potent. She caught her breath and felt her heartbeat trip once, then resume its heavy beat. Her emotions now were different from the ones she'd felt the other night. Perhaps it was the unrelenting sunlight that bathed them, allowing no hidden expressions, no secrets, to come between them.

He half knelt astride her. Entwining their fingers, he raised her hands to either side of her head. The action lifted her breasts and he dipped his head to lick first one rosy nipple, then the other. She moaned softly at the sensation, warm and sure, that surged through her, and lifted her upper body toward his mouth.

Hamp accepted her invitation, using his tongue, his lips, tasting the film of perspiration that lay lightly on her skin, until he was drowning in the sensual heat that scented her body. He lifted his head to pin her with a hot gaze, to judge her readiness. Her eyes were mere slits of gleaming emerald, her breath escaped in small gasps through slightly parted lips. He felt a glorious realization surge through his loins, endangering his already thin control—that he could bring her to this, that she could want him so, that her desire could be equally as powerful as his.

She opened to him.

Hamp's powerful thrust was a shock at first, unlike the slow, easy blending of their bodies before. But, with an unmistakable effort at control, he slowed, allowing her to adapt to the feel of him inside her again, then to take all of him.

The sky above was endless; the music of the sea rebounded through her, echoing the rhythm of his movements, the waves increasing, expanding, building with each lunge. Suddenly she tensed, clinging to his shoulders, holding her breath, waiting for the ultimate undulation to sweep over her, to saturate her with mindless feeling. And then it came, crashing over her, setting off climactic seizures of the most wondrous excitement she had ever known.

"Dani, oh, Dani, my love," he whispered as he joined her at the pinnacle. Then he, too, was spun into the vortex, his breath pushed from him as though by a giant hand, leaving him gasping, shuddering in her arms.

Later they laughed as they scrambled around in the sand to hunt for his glasses. Dani decided the sound of laughter was the most incredible accompaniment to romance.

They waded into the sea. Hamp scooped handfuls of water over her, washing away the sand. Then he licked the sparkling droplets from her bare breasts, her belly, her thighs. They played a sensual game of tag in the warmth of the sun and made love again at the edge of the world. They walked naked under the palm trees, as Adam and Eve might have walked in the Garden of Eden before they were expelled from paradise.

Man and woman, together in a perfect time, a perfect place. If there were never to be another, this one was enough, Dani told herself, and almost believed it. But a small voice inside would not be quelled. Would she still believe this moment was worth it tomorrow night, when they boarded the airplane that would return them to the real world?

The exile that she and Hamp faced after this was over was their own choice, born of their own circumstances. She shrugged off an intrusive thought that she might regret the brief glimpse into heaven.

Hamp watched and thought how beautiful she was, strolling like a naked nymph through a tropical forest. As they left the protection of one tree for another, the sunlight caressed her fleetingly, like a lover intent on arousal, teasing her breast, her cheek, her thigh. But there was sadness in her eyes, which reflected his own growing melancholy. The idyllic day was drawing to a close. Soon they would have to return to the hotel, to the children.

"Hamp!" His name was a cry on her lips. He turned and she was there suddenly, throwing her arms around his neck. He knew her thoughts followed his own. This time when they made love it was with a desperation and hunger that would not be appeased.

"WHAT PUT THE SADNESS in your eyes?" he asked over the purr of the outrigger's motor.

"It's been a wonderful day, one I'll never forget," she answered lightly, arranging her hat to shield her face from the sun. "I'm just thinking of the hundreds of things I have to do when we get home."

"Yeah. Me, too." Hamp's fingers tightened on the handle of the motor. "You know, this seat's wide enough for us both," he said. "Come on over here."

She went promptly, smiling.

He smiled back and gave her a hug. "Listen, Dani, I've been thinking. I don't want this to end here. Can't we continue to see each other?"

Dani's smile faded. She had already worked her feelings out with her conscience and now he came up with this horrible suggestion. A lingering parting would be much worse than a clean break—but she decided not to say so directly. "Sure. We live in the same area. We're bound to run into each other."

"That wasn't what I meant, and you know it," he said shortly.

"Hamp, we've discussed this. We're too different, you and I. A relationship wouldn't be practical."

"I know we've discussed it, dammit. And I know we agreed that our attraction is a vacation fling. But what if it isn't? The real world is about to descend on us again. But Dani, I don't want to write off what we have shared today. I want to continue to see you, to be with you."

When? she wanted to demand. *I work at night; you work in the daytime. I like hot dogs; you prefer Châteaubriand. You live in a huge house and love it because you can entertain; I live in an apartment and love it because I don't have much to clean. You go into San Francisco for the opera; I go to the wharf.*

But again she kept silent, wondering herself if it were possible, if she even wanted it to be possible. Suddenly she was uncomfortably aware of her own inclinations and had a clear answer to her own, earlier, questions.

Making love with Hamp had been a big mistake if it could provoke even the contemplation of such possibilities. She made her own decisions, was her own person; she'd worked long and hard to achieve independence. She didn't cater to the schedule or the whims of anyone else, except David of course, although his demands had always been more on himself than on her.

If a few days spent in paradise with this man could cause her to question her life-style, then even a few days had been a dreadful mistake.

They had reached the dock. While Hamp was settling up with the man who'd rented them the outrigger, she turned for a last look at the *motu* in the distance. The sea, which had been calm this morning, had begun to dip and swell as though a giant beneath the surface were stretching himself after a long sleep.

"You're holding something back," Hamp said when he joined her.

She turned to face him fully. "Yes, I'm holding something back, a part of me that I can't share. You recognize it because you're the same kind of person, with the same feelings. You're holding back, too. You have been ever since we got to Huahine."

No, just since the night you were sunburned— Hamp amended her words in his mind. *That was when I realized just how vulnerable I am to you, how deep my feelings go.* He knew that this wasn't the time to confess to either his roller coaster feelings, joy-filled one moment, wistful the next, or the reasons for his guardedness.

"I'm not criticizing you for it, Hamp." She picked up the white shirt and pulled it on over her bathing suit. "I understand because we're alike. I can't give too much of myself, and neither can you. It's a mistake for either of us to ask that of ourselves." She wrapped the shirt around her, holding it closed with arms crossed protectively over her stomach.

"If I call you, will you refuse to see me?"

"Of course not," she said, sighing heavily.

It wasn't enough, but he had a feeling it was all he'd get for now.

This wasn't the time to tell her that he was in love with her. But it was the time to admit it to himself. His mouth hardened to a firm and determined line of resolution. Soon, he vowed, very soon.

8

ON SUNDAY, less than two days later, Dani dragged herself out of bed at twelve noon and plugged the telephone back in. Back to the real world with a bang, she'd thought when she'd finally arrived home from the club a bit after four in the morning.

Saturday night was always busy, and to add to that, she had been slightly out of sync with the routine. There had been the bills to pay, the food and liquor orders to draw up for the next week. The manager, who had been with her for only six months, was working out well. He had run things efficiently in her absence, so she'd given him the night off.

She needed a vacation to recover from her vacation, she told herself. She had only taken two steps when the phone rang. "Hello," she said, her voice still thick with the traces of sleep.

"Dani, where the hell have you been? I've been calling all morning."

See? she told herself. See what happens when you have to answer to someone else? She tried to work up some enthusiasm but she was too tired. "Good morning, Hamp."

Still, the effort it took must have come through. He laughed, that warm, sexy chuckle. "Morning?" he questioned gently. "It's afternoon, honey. Did I wake you?"

She smothered a yawn. "No. But five minutes ago you would have."

"Did the club survive your absence?"

She yawned again. "I guess so. I didn't get in until after four."

"Four in the morning?" he asked, his voice strong with disapproval. "We just got home yesterday morning. I thought you'd take some time to rest from the flight before plunging back in full strength."

"Yesterday was Saturday," she reminded him. "Saturday is our busiest night."

"But you—" He bit off what he'd been about to say. "Listen, honey," he continued after a pause. "My summer-school classes start tomorrow. I'm going to be tied up night and day during the week. I wondered if we could have dinner tonight."

"Tonight?" Sunday? Sunday was her day to clean, and this Sunday was worse than most. With a sinking heart she looked around. The apartment was a mess, it hadn't been vacuumed or dusted, and she had vacation laundry to do.

But she longed to see him. She missed him. After only two days? she asked herself disgustedly.

Two days ago they were making love on an uninhabited island. Later, after returning to the hotel, they had sat in the cocktail lounge and talked late into the night, arguing, discussing, rationalizing. And their final decision hadn't been a conclusive one at all; it had been more of a compromise, waiting to see what happened when they got home.

"Okay," said Dani. "Tonight is fine. But I don't feel like going out. I'll order in and we can eat here. Do you like Chinese?"

Another pause. He was probably thinking in terms of some intimate little romantic restaurant. "Don't bother ordering," he said. "I'll pick up something on my way. Seven?"

"Seven o'clock," she agreed. "See you then."

The rest of the afternoon was spent racing around the apartment. David wandered in around six wearing a wet bathing suit and informed her he had been at a friend's pool all day. Tonight he was going out for pizza with Carole Anne.

Dani was pleased that his vacation mood seemed to have lingered. Maybe he was beginning to loosen the tight strings he held on himself. "A whole day of loafing? I'm impressed," she teased, careful to show her pleasure.

He shrugged, noticing for the first time the results of her labor. "Hey, Mom. The place looks great."

"Thank you, David," answered Dani dryly. Neither of them ever placed much importance on a spotless house. They shared tasks and as long as things were reasonably clean and picked up, they were satisfied. So she was sure he knew the reason, but she told him anyway. "Hamp is coming over."

He grinned. "I wondered."

"Scat!" she told him, swiping at his bare legs with a dish towel.

"I'm going! I'm going!" He disappeared into his bathroom. Reminding herself to check for wet towels when he finished, she headed for her own room, stripping the scarf off her hair as she went.

Forty-five minutes later they met in the living room again. Dani had showered, shampooed her hair and done her nails, congratulating herself on a new speed record. She wore spotless white sharkskin slacks and a white silk blouse. Around her waist was an emerald green sash, tied obi style. Anyone looking at her would never have known that she hadn't lounged by the pool all day.

David greeted her with a wolf whistle and Dani studied him fondly, wondering where he'd picked that up. She was savvy enough to know that wolf whistles had gone out with the Beatles. "Thanks, dear. It was clever of you to find a clean pair of jeans," she congratulated him.

"Yeah, I noticed you haven't finished the laundry," he said, distracted by a sudden thought. "Mom, is Sandy coming with Hamp?"

"Oh, drat." She flew to the telephone and dialed Hamp's number. "I was so sleepy when I talked to him I forgot to ask. I wouldn't want her to think she isn't welcome." She counted the rings—seven, eight. The number didn't answer. She hung up. "At least she isn't at home alone."

"Why don't I stick around until he gets here, just in case."

She looked at him blankly. "Just in case what?"

"In case he brings her with him, Mom," he explained patiently. "You wouldn't want her hanging around. You know Carole Anne. This date's kind of a casual thing. Sandy could tag along."

Dani let the silence stretch. Not about to comment on the first part of his statement, she considered the second, tapping her chin thoughtfully with a freshly manicured nail. Finally she spoke. "David, do you like Sandy?"

"Sure, I like her," he answered casually.

"I mean do you *like* her?"

He turned away from the stereo, where he had been flipping through the albums. "Mom," he said patiently. "Sandy's just a kid. We're friends, that's all. Brother-sister friends. We're too different for there ever to be a romantic relationship between us."

Dani's eyes widened. *I know what you mean,* she concurred silently. "You didn't get along very well at first," she said tentatively.

He nodded. "She can be a real pain in the ass sometimes. Especially when she puts on those la-di-da New York airs. But I think I've gotten her cued in to the way we do things in California."

"David," she said, the admonition clear in her tone. "That isn't—" The doorbell sounded, cutting off anything more Dani might have intended to say.

David went through to the small entrance hall to answer it. "Hi, Hamp." She heard him greet the man cheerfully. "You alone?"

There was a low answer of more than one word.

"I've got to pick up my date at seven-thirty. See you. Bye, Mom," he called back.

Hamp entered the room and Dani's hands were suddenly damp. He looked fantastic in linen slacks and a blue dress shirt with its sleeves rolled back over his muscular forearms. "Bye, David," she said hoarsely after the door had closed. She waited where she was, nervous for some reason. She had to say something. "Hi."

"Hi, yourself," said Hamp.

She wiped her hands on her white sharkskin pants. What would he think of her home? She could imagine the comparison. The residential area where he lived was one of the most exclusive in a city of exclusive homes. She remembered wide lawns, perfectly manicured, huge houses set way back from the street, large old trees.

She looked fantastic, thought Hamp. Had she been this beautiful in Tahiti? Had her waist been that tiny? Did her hair, loose around her shoulders, shine like this? Hamp roused himself from the stupor that had descended upon him. He carried two large paper bags, one in each hand. As he approached he transferred one of them, leaving a hand free to touch her cheek. "Hi," he repeated softly as he bent his head to brush her lips with his.

There was an awkward pause. Wondering at its cause, and oddly unsure of himself, he dropped his hand, looked around. "This is nice," he said.

The apartment was a reflection of her, lots of light, small, efficient, slashes of color—vivid scarlet, bold blue, rich green. The living room was not large, but not cramped, either. At ground level, its French doors led out onto a small lawn surrounded by a head height redwood fence.

The room was furnished with suitable, if not remarkable, furniture. A deep blue sofa, selected for comfort and piled with pillows, had been placed in the middle of the room to define the dining area. Two easy chairs, also comfortable looking, sat at angles to the sofa. A wall of shelves contained a stereo, a television, and books—hundreds of books—the unit didn't look as though it could hold one more. A pass-through counter indicated the location of the kitchen. Beyond the entrance he'd noticed a hall that he presumed led to the bedrooms. He wondered what kind of bed she slept in.

He spared a fleeting thought for his own home. This whole apartment would have fit into his living room. He frowned. His house was much too big for two people, three with the housekeeper, but she had her own apartment.

Dani misunderstood the frown. "It's nothing fancy," she said, lifting her chin to a level just lower than supercilious. "But it's perfect for David and me."

"I'm sure it is," said Hamp.

"We were lucky to get a ground-floor unit. We have lots of privacy with the fence." Lord, she was chattering like a spinster on her first date.

Something was wrong, very wrong, thought Hamp. Within the space of a few sentences she had let him know right off that he was the intruder here. He sighed. What had he expected? He'd known it wasn't going to be easy. He hadn't insulted her taste, had he? "I like it. Could I get rid of this?" He held up the two bags.

"Oh, dear. Of course. Here, let me take them."

"No, just direct me to the kitchen."

"This way." Dani realized that she was now the one who hid behind formality. "I suppose we should eat while it's hot. Would you like something to drink first?"

"Scotch, if you have it," he said.

Dani turned stricken eyes to him. "I'm sorry, Hamp. All I have is a rather unremarkable wine."

Her strained expression was so unlike the Dani he knew, Hamp dropped the bags on the counter and reached for her, recognizing instinctively and correctly what was troubling her. He should have known sooner. The differences in their life-styles had been one of her major arguments against continuing this relationship. "Hey, honey, it's me. Remember? I don't give a damn what we drink."

She went into his arms. "I know who you are. You're Hampton Lowell the Third. See? I told you it wouldn't work! I told you—"

He dipped his head, caught her lips, smothering any further words. "Shut up," he told her affectionately, when he finally lifted his head. "We haven't been home two full days yet and already you're throwing up barriers. Give it a chance, Dani. Give *us* a chance."

Dani slid her arms up to wind them around his neck. She positioned her face in the spot under his chin where she could most easily inhale the delicious scent of him. "You're right. I'm tired and I worked so damned hard to clean up this place, when all I wanted to do today was be a couch potato."

Familiar with the descriptive term, one of Sandy's favorites when she wanted to be lazy, he chuckled. He stroked her back, his long fingers moving in a comforting massage. "You should have told me, honey. I don't give a damn what your apartment looks like. I can barely see it anyway for looking at you. I've missed you like hell," he finished, dipping again toward her lips.

"I've missed you, too." Dani stood on her toes to answer the kiss warmly. She slid her fingers into the hair at the back of his head. Her lips parted; her tongue met his. With a sigh she melted against him, giving herself to the wonderful sensation of being held by him again.

Hamp felt his arousal grow insistent. Almost desperately he tried to erase the memory of her naked body on the sand. He could think of nothing he wanted as much as he wanted to take Dani down the hall to her bedroom, strip the clothes from her body, lay her down on whatever kind of bed he found there and make long, delicious love to her. But he restrained himself, loosening the bonds of his embrace. The affinity between them was fragile, right now. If he were to convince her of his love he must go slowly, help her to be sure that sex was not all he wanted from her, or to give her.

He combed his fingers into her hair and, using his thumbs, raised her face for a study. Her green eyes were slumberous as she looked back at him; a phantom smile curved her lips. A stray wisp of flame curled around his forefinger, like a binding silken tendril. He felt the most engulfing surge of emotion well up in him, threatening his carefully planned pact with himself not to overwhelm her with his own feelings. Once he had admitted his love to himself, it seemed to have grown by leaps and bounds, with each hour, each minute. He had never loved like this. Surely no one who had ever lived had ever loved this deeply, this strongly, this completely.

He kissed her eyebrows, the tip of her nose, her cheeks, tenderly, lovingly. "Dani—" The telephone on the wall behind them rang, exploding the gentle moment. Expelling the breath he'd been holding, he twisted around to pick up the receiver and handed it to her.

Dani gripped the receiver with a strangling hold. There was something in Hamp's eyes that she hadn't had time to fully examine. "Hello," she said quickly, holding on to his gaze, anxious to get rid of whoever it was. "Oh, hi, Elizabeth." The call was from one of her friends, who wanted to hear all about Tahiti.

She shrugged helplessly, but she knew the mood was broken.

Hamp turned away to busy himself with the food he'd brought, resisting the yen to swear at the unknown woman. This was the world away from paradise; it was this world they had to cope with if there was to be anything between them. The interruption had come at a propitious time. He'd been on the verge of pushing and, knowing Dani Fox, she would have pushed right back. The timing was all wrong. It was too soon. If anything, he should be thanking the woman on the other end of the line.

Elizabeth was a dear, but Dani had never realized what a chatterbox she was. Finally she managed to interrupt the flow. "Elizabeth, I have company. I'll call you tomorrow and tell you all about the trip," she said and hung up, her fingers clinging to the receiver for an instant. "Are you finding everything? Good heavens, Hamp. That's enough food for an army!" She laughed at the array of cartons.

Hamp met her smile with an easy grin. "I'm hungry. Where are your plates?"

She took them from the cabinet, place mats and paper napkins from a drawer and led the way into the dining area. "I forgot to ask, where is Sandy?"

"She had a date with Rocky II," he grumbled, depositing two cartons on the table. He went back for the others.

"David offered to take her along with him tonight. Did you decide what you want to drink?" she asked, reentering the kitchen. While he put the rest of the food on the table, she opened the refrigerator and looked inside. "How about milk?"

"Milk is fine. David did?" he said speculatively. "Interesting. He told me he had a date."

She poured two glasses of milk, found serving spoons and joined him at the table. "He did. I thought the same thing you're thinking, so I asked him. He assured me that they were good friends, but there was nothing romantic between them." She dished rice onto her plate.

"I suppose she's too young for David," said Hamp, real regret coloring his voice. He sighed, returning his full attention to the woman across the table. "I have to be home at midnight, by the way," he said with a suggestive grin. "Can you think of something to fill the hours?"

Efficiently she stripped the paper off her chopsticks and broke them apart. "Besides eating Chinese while it's still hot, you mean?"

His dark eyes gleamed, and he brought his chair around to wedge it next to hers. "Yeah, besides that."

Looking at him over her first bite with wide, innocent eyes, she said, "I thought you were hungry. I am. Eat your dinner, Hamp. We'll think about other things later."

"You're a cruel woman," he teased. Laying his arm across the back of her chair, he leaned forward to grasp her hand. He redirected her bite to his mouth and began to play with her hair. "I need a fork," he said when he'd finished chewing.

"A fork," she scoffed, unsteadily. His hand in her hair was beginning to have its effect. She felt her body grow lethargic. "I never figured you for a faintheart, Professor."

"Oh, but I am," he said with feeling.

The remark brought her questioning gaze to his. He smiled. "If you won't give me a fork, you can feed me." He pointed to a serving of steak and peppers on her plate. "Some of that."

"Okay." Maneuvering the chopsticks wasn't as easy as it had been. She held out the bite, her free hand underneath to catch the drips.

Hamp caught her hand as he took the bite. Holding her eyes, he chewed and swallowed; then he licked the tiny drop of sauce from her palm, his tongue lingering long after the drip was gone.

She was shaking like a leaf in an autumn storm by the time he'd finished. She cleared her throat. "Now, may I have some?"

He smiled, tracing her jawline with a knuckle. "Yeah."

Slowly, sensually, they shared the chopsticks, working their way through the almond chicken and sweet-and-sour shrimp. Dani let the heat take her, flow through her body, searching out every nerve end, every crevice.

When Hamp's hand burrowed beneath her hair to caress her nape, Dani's movements grew indolent with desire. "That feels good," she said huskily, her body drawn toward his in hunger and anticipation as though it were a magnet and she, the flimsiest shred of metal filing.

"Does it?" he murmured with a small smile, feeling the pull of her hypnotic green eyes. "You know, Dani, my memories of making love to you on the *motu*, are beginning to haunt me. I'll be doing something else, reading, talking on the phone, and suddenly I remember how the sun looked on your hair."

"I haven't been able to forget, either," she admitted softly. "Last night, I was discussing some changes in the menu with the chef. My thoughts just stopped on me. The poor man thought I'd lost my mind."

His lips hovered only a breath away, her blood had begun to sing in expectation of his kiss, when the sound of a key in the lock brought both their heads around with a jerk.

David entered the room, a thoroughly disgusted look on his face. His steps halted at the sight of them. Then he moved on. "Sorry. Carole Anne got a better offer. You guys just go on with whatever you were doing. I'm going to my room." He disappeared down the hall.

Neither of them moved until they heard his door close. Then Dani let out a sigh that seemed to have been born in her toes. "Well, damn," she said.

Hamp laughed. It was a weak sound because he'd never felt less like laughing, but he made the attempt. "It is his home, honey."

"I know." She rested her head on his shoulder. "Hamp, I don't know how to say this...."

Squeezing his eyes shut, he kissed the top of her head, loving her so much. "I'll say it for you," he offered tenderly. "You're tired. You won't make love with David in the apartment. You're sorry, but could we call it a night? Have I covered everything?"

She nodded and tilted her head back to look at him. "Everything except my regret that the evening had to end this way," she said softly, sincerely.

He gave her a short, hard kiss—anything else was beyond him. "Do you want me to help you clean this up?" he asked, indicating the remains of their meal.

"No, I'll call David in and turn him loose on the leftovers."

"I'll say good-night then," he said. He stood, drawing her under his arm and walked slowly toward the door. Dani matched her steps to his, dejection pulling down the corners of her mouth.

In the small hallway he stopped, wondering at the wisdom of what he was about to do. Would she think he was pushing too hard? Concluding that it was another hurdle, one of many, he did it anyway. "I'm having a party at my house two weeks from today. I'd like for you to act as my hostess. Will you?"

"What kind of party?" she asked, hesitating.

"A cocktail party, a pretty big one," he admitted. "I do this every year. Invite friends and faculty. It starts at six and is usually over by nine. My brother Larry is coming with his wife, and the sweetheart of our family, my Aunt Delores. I'd like for you to meet them, and them, you."

Not missing the significance of the invitation, Dani knew a moment's dread. Home to meet the family. Larry Lawrence, the Lowell newspaperman who had caused her such grief. Sometimes she was even able to forget, but that wouldn't be the case if they met face-to-face in Hamp's house. "Shouldn't Aunt Delores act as your hostess? Or Sandy?" she asked evasively.

"Sandy's going to New York next week to visit her grandparents. She won't get home until late the evening of the party. Will you?"

"I guess so," she said slowly, hesitating to accept this responsibility but unable to decline.

The pulse at the base of her throat had begun to beat visibly. "You don't sound very enthusiastic," Hamp accused lightly. "The party is on a Sunday, so the club will be closed."

Was he hurt by her reluctance? Dani looked up, wanting him to understand that her unwillingness didn't have anything to do with him. She smiled and laid her hand on his chest for balance while she raised on her toes to kiss him lightly. "My lack of enthusiasm is due to the fact that most of the entertaining I do is the backyard-barbecue kind," she explained. "I may be a disappointment to you."

She hadn't realized how tense he was, waiting for her answer until she felt him relax.

Smiling, Hamp linked his hands loosely behind her back. "You couldn't disappoint me if you tried. The caterers will see to the food, the bartenders will mix the drinks, all you have to do is show up looking beautiful. And that won't be a problem for you at all."

THE NEXT WEEK sped by at a hectic pace.

Dani had accomplished something she'd promised herself she would do as soon as she got home. She had called the booking agent on Monday.

"Jimmy, I want to start auditioning for a permanent singer for the club or, if you can't find 'forever' permanent, someone who will sign at least a year's contract."

She had been making do with two- and three-week bookings, filling in herself when money was tight. She seldom performed anymore, but occasionally, on a weekend, she would be called into service if Jimmy couldn't find a really good talent. The business side of the club seemed to take more and more of her time and attention.

The agent hesitated. "I have someone who might be exactly who you're looking for. A woman who recently moved up from L.A. came to see me a few weeks ago, name of Geraldine Griffin, calls herself GG. A long-term contract would probably appeal to her. She's terrific. Only trouble is, last time I saw her, she was pregnant."

He said the word as though it were a disease. Dani laughed. She could imagine the rotund man chewing on his cigar, looking down his nose at an entertainer who would be so careless as to let herself get in that condition. "How pregnant is she?"

"Very."

"Well, it isn't a permanent disability, you know."

"Yeah, I think I remember my mother telling me something like that."

"You had a mother?" teased Dani.

He grumped for a minute. "Lemme just look at her file. Yeah, here you go." He was quiet for a minute. "Tell you what, I'll send her tape over to you and you can listen. I'd really hate to get her hopes up if there's no chance."

Dani's jaw dropped. "He has a heart, too," she said.

"Sometimes," he agreed.

The tape arrived soon after lunch. Dani ran it on the small machine in her office, turning the volume up high. The tones of a rich contralto voice filled the room, its bluesy tones catching her interest. In less than eight bars, she knew she had found exactly what she wanted. In less than sixteen, her manager stuck his head in the door. "Hire her. That is, if you're looking for a singer."

She called Jimmy immediately and later that night he called back. "Good news, Dani. She's not pregnant anymore." The audition was set for the next day.

THE MEMBERS of the band were grinning; the kitchen help were peering through the glass strip in the door. "When can you start?" Dani asked the striking black woman as the last notes faded away.

The relief that softened the woman's features almost brought tears to her eyes. She remembered the feeling well.

"Yesterday," said GG.

Dani grinned. "I know what you mean. Come back to my office and we'll discuss salary."

They came to an agreement that suited them both. "Now, when can you start?" Dani asked again.

GG hesitated. "I ought to tell you, I don't have a hus-band." She waited, as though she expected Dani to make some remark. When Dani merely raised an inquiring brow, she went on, "I have to find someone to stay with Nichole, my baby."

Dani tore a piece of paper off the pad at her elbow and scrawled a name and number on it. "Try this woman. Her name is Mrs. Henderson. She kept my son for me when he was a baby. If she's still sitting, you'll love her."

GG rose and extended her hand. "Thank you so much, Mrs. Fox. You don't know how indebted to you I am."

Dani covered their clasped hands with her other one and grinned. "Call me Dani. Someday I'll tell you the story of how I got started in this business." She dropped the wom-an's hand and picked up the pad again. "Let me see. I need a couple of days to get something in the newspaper, and Jimmy will have to draw up the contracts. You'll need time to rehearse. Can you come in the mornings?" She nodded with satisfaction at the affirmative answer. "Let's aim for a Saturday opening. That's our heaviest night, of course, and it will give you a good audience. Now, about your cos-tumes—I can give you an advance if you need one—"

Dani finally got the grateful woman out of her office and called Hamp. "She's starting Saturday. You have to come, Hamp. She's terrific."

"I'd rather be alone with you," Hamp muttered with gruff amusement. The sound of her voice over an insular appa-ratus didn't do a damned thing except add to his frustra-tion. "Honey, I'm beginning to get very puckered around the fingertips."

Dani laughed, but she fully understood what he meant. On the nights during the week, when she could leave the club early, he had set up evening classes for summer stu-dents who worked during the day. Afterward he kept his office open for counseling sessions. They had talked on the phone daily, but it wasn't enough for either of them. And there were always the kids.

"Sandy leaves Saturday for a visit with her grandparents," he said, as though he'd read her mind.

Her heart leaped at the suggestion. Alone—they could be alone. But then it resumed its regular beat. She couldn't possibly desert her new singer on her first night. "Come and hear GG Saturday night and after dinner maybe we can sneak out early," she offered.

"If she's that good . . ."

"She *is* that good. And I have to be there for her opening, Hamp. You do understand, don't you?"

He sighed audibly. "Yeah, I understand."

DANI KNEW this Saturday was going to be a bad night from the first minute she arrived at the club. A grim-faced Gary, her manager, held out the telephone receiver. GG was on the line. "Mrs. Henderson just called. Nichole has a temperature and has broken out in a rash. I have to pick her up right away. Oh, Dani, I don't know what to say."

Damn. She should never have forgotten Murphy's Law. The rehearsals had gone so well; the ads she'd placed in the papers had reaped their reward: a full book of reservations. She soothed the singer as best she could, swallowing her own disappointment, and hung up only to be informed by her manager, that one of the bartenders had also called in sick. "We can't handle a Saturday-night crowd with only one bartender."

"I know that," snapped Dani, then regretted her shortness. "Sorry, Gary. What do you suggest?"

When Hamp arrived at eight o'clock, she pulled him into her office, closed the door and went into his arms. "You may be sorry you came," she said shakily when she emerged from his deep kiss. "Just about everything that could go wrong, has gone wrong tonight."

He smiled tenderly, holding her, combing through her hair with his fingers as she told him about GG and the bartender and Murphy's Law. He chuckled; his mouth rested briefly on her forehead. "I wanted to see you," he said simply. "No, I *needed* to see you. If this is where you are, this is where I want to be."

"I hope you have a good supply of patience," she warned. "Now, get out of here while I change."

"Can't I help?" he asked with a wolfish grin.

"Do you think we'd make it out of this room?"

"I guess you're right," he conceded, but he pulled her into his arms for one more kiss.

After changing into one of her show outfits, a clinging gold lamé sheath, she checked to make sure Gary had put Hamp at the best table, right beside the dance floor. She headed across the room to join him there for a minute.

He rose at her approach and she felt an unfamiliar pressure in her chest, which was almost a pain. He was certainly not the only man in the club wearing a tuxedo, but few of the others wore them with such familiarity and comfort. None of the others had such broad shoulders, such lean hips.

His gaze roamed over her. He seemed a little bit disconcerted, but then he smiled—a warm, intimate smile that touched a sweet chord somewhere deep inside her. He held out his hand in a perfectly natural gesture. She put hers into it, feeling that something meaningful had happened between one instant and another. She swallowed a gasp, realizing that at this minute—had he asked—she could have walked out of her club and never looked back.

But she didn't have time to analyze her response. She wanted to stand there and drink in the sight of him, but there wasn't time to do that, either.

"I can't stay but a minute," she said, slipping into the seat next to him. "Have the prime rib," she suggested, huskily. "It's wonderful."

Hamp linked their fingers firmly to reassure himself that this woman in the seductive gown with the heavy makeup was his Dani. She smelled the same, like a French summer, her voice was the same: low and exciting. But her eyes were drawn with an exotic hand and her lips were meltingly but falsely glossy. He didn't like the image she projected. "Aren't you going to have dinner?" he asked, attempting to keep his conflicting emotions out of his tone.

She nodded, noticing his response to her stage persona. His roving eyes took in everything again, this time in great detail, leaving her weak with regret. "I'll join you after the first set. I promise."

And she fully intended to keep her promise. But there always seemed to be a question that had to be answered, a decision to be made, and she was the only one to provide her customers with entertainment. He had been left sitting alone most of the hour and a half he'd been there.

After Dani's second set, she joined him, breathless. A waiter had been watching, and as soon as she was seated he brought her seafood cocktail. "Wonderful. I'm starving." She took a bite. There was shell in the crabmeat. She called the waiter back. "Take this to the kitchen and tell them not to serve another until the crabmeat has been picked carefully," she said imperiously, handing over the plate. "If the chef gives you trouble, show him this." She pointed to a tiny, transparent fragment on the rim of the plate.

The waiter nodded. "Yes, ma'am."

"Tough lady," Hamp observed with a small smile. "Seems I said that once before."

She shot him a smile in return. "I have to be. But sometimes I wish I'd never started serving a full dinner menu." The club had only been equipped to serve light supper items when she'd bought half from Schyler. It was one of the things they'd argued over heatedly.

"Mine was delicious."

Dani looked up, intending to respond, but over Hamp's shoulder she saw her manager coming toward their table. She gave an audible groan. "I should have put you in a table in the back corner. What now?" she muttered under her breath.

Hamp glanced around. He was becoming very familiar with the man who approached. Instead of ignoring him, however, he pulled out the empty chair adjacent to his own. "Won't you join us?" he asked smoothly.

Dani's eyes darted to his face, searching for sarcasm, but she found none. Gary waited for her nod. "Sit down, Gary. Has something else happened?"

"The kid who said he'd worked as a bartender? Well, I think the experience he bragged about was in a fraternity house. He's already used bourbon in two martinis and Scotch in a piña colada."

Hamp rubbed a broad hand over his mouth, but not in time to hide a grin. His brown eyes sparked with amusement behind his glasses.

Dani looked at him sharply. "It isn't funny, Hamp," she said sternly. Her sense of humor had somehow deserted her over the past few hours.

He raised his brows and sobered immediately. "I'm not laughing, Dani."

Gary looked from one of them to the other. "Do you want me to take over?" he asked finally.

"No, you can't be at the front and back at the same time. I'll—"

"I mix a pretty good drink," said Hamp.

Both heads swiveled, both pairs of eyes stared. Dani studied him the longest. "Union scale," she said at last.

One corner of his mouth lifted. "I could probably hold you up for double."

"Not a chance," she shot back. "I'd sing from behind the bar first."

Hamp tongued his cheek. "As I said before, tough lady."

Dani didn't feel tough, she felt wary; but she really didn't have a choice unless she did as she threatened—tended bar while she sang. Maybe she could stand on her head, too.

It was nearly midnight before things calmed down enough for Dani to take a break when the band did. She joined Hamp behind the bar. He was polishing glasses. The canned music coming through the speakers over the bar was too loud. She adjusted the volume before she asked, "How are things going?" She was hesitant, not at all encouraged by his expression.

He shrugged, sliding the last glass into the overhead wooden rack.

"Thank you for pitching in to help."

"You're welcome." Hamp knew he sounded surly, but he couldn't help himself. He'd held in there all evening, smiling politely, fending off a few propositions, cleaning up spilled drinks, until some damned drunk, after accusing him of watering the gin, wanted to fight. He'd assisted the man to the back door with less than a careful hand and felt a great satisfaction doing so.

Then he had asked himself what in the hell was he doing here.

"I warned you I should have put you at a table in the back corner," said Dani, lightly, in an effort to diffuse his temper.

"Yeah," he said, no laughter in his voice at all. "Then you could have just forgotten I was here."

Wordlessly she looked at him. He had removed his black dinner jacket. His tie was still knotted and his pleated dress shirt molded his shoulders to perfection. But, she noticed, the cuffs were stained. "Some nights are like this," she said quietly. "I'm sorry you were subjected to one of them."

In no mood to be mollified, Hamp searched her features. She was on the edge, exhausted. "Then you ought to get into another line of work. Hold out your hand."

When she didn't comply he grabbed her wrist. "Look at you. You're shaking like a leaf," he accused harshly.

Dani looked at her fingers as though they belonged to someone else. She hadn't even been aware of their trembling, but she wasn't particularly alarmed. "It's stage fright," she said. "I've always had it. Even when I sang at the club in Tahiti my hands were shaking. It'll stop as soon as the last set is finished."

Hamp made an angry noise, something between a snort and a sneer. As he'd watched her being run to a frazzle, he felt the anger building in him. It was an irrational reaction. He knew she had her duties to perform, he'd known she'd be busy. But, rational or not, it was there.

His inarticulate response brought out her own anger. "Why did you volunteer to help, why did you even come if you're going to act like an adolescent?" She regretted the words as soon as they were out. She'd been desperate and he'd pitched in to help her. How could she have said such a thing?

"Vodka and tonic, please," said a stylishly dressed woman who had approached, unnoticed by either of them. "With a twist of lemon," she added, smiling openly at the handsome man tending bar.

Hamp sent Dani a look before returning the woman's smile politely. He placed a cocktail napkin on the shining mahogany, took down a glass and scooped ice into it. Upending the vodka bottle, he gave the drink a hefty shot.

Dani dragged her hand through her hair. Lord, she was tired. "I'm sorry," she apologized in a soft tone. "I shouldn't have said that."

A muscle in his jaw jerked as he sloshed tonic into the glass.

"Do you have lime instead of lemon?" asked the woman.

"Certainly," answered Hamp. He reached for a wedge of lime and a plastic stirrer.

"I said I was sorry," said Dani.

"Are you running a tab?" he asked the woman as he placed the drink in front of her.

She looked from one of them to the other interestedly and pointed to a nearby table. He nodded as he moved to ring up the cost of the drink. "An apology is unnecessary. I wanted to be with you," he said in a low voice to Dani.

"Well, you're with me," she snapped again. "Do you like it?"

He slapped at the long button of the cash register with his open palm. The machine responded with a merry tinkle and efficiently spat a ticket into his waiting hand. "No, I don't. Not one damned bit."

"Dani," said Gary's voice from behind her. "One of the waiters rang up five hundred bowls of clam chowder instead of five. Do you want me to straighten out the register or do you want to do it?"

"Could I have another smidgen of lime?" asked the woman in a coy little voice.

Dani couldn't take much more of this. She grabbed the lime herself and slammed it down on the bar, where it squirted all over the polished surface. Then she spun on her heel and marched away.

THE NEXT MORNING Dani rose at the crack of dawn. She made herself wait until eight o'clock to call Hamp. She let the phone ring ten times before she hung up, only to try again five minutes later.

She was on the third try when the doorbell rang. She looked through the peephole to see Hamp there, his arms filled with flowers. Dani flung the door open and stood like a stone, looking at him helplessly, her emotions vacillating between hope and despair. "I've been trying to call you."

"Dani, I'm sorry. I was a bear," he murmured, folding her into his arms, the flowers crushed between them. The scent of broken petals drifted up from the bouquet.

"No, I'm the one who should be sorry. I took advantage of you. Then I came at you like a shrew."

"No, no, I won't listen to that." Hungrily he covered her lips with his. But the huge bouquet kept them apart.

Smiling against his lips, Dani pulled back. "It appears you brought me flowers."

Hamp looked down as though he'd never seen them before.

She took his hand. "Come in. I'll put them in water and fix us some coffee. We have to talk, Hamp." When the flowers were arranged and coffee was dripping into the carafe, she turned to face him. Propping one hip against the counter, she plunged her hands into the pockets of her old terry-cloth robe.

He looked as tired as she felt. The lines around his eyes were more pronounced than they'd been last week. She tightened her belt, preparing to open the conversation, intending to be honest about her feelings for him and what she saw as problems without solutions.

Hamp spoke before she could. "I love you, Dani."

Dani closed her eyes. Her hands clenched inside the pockets. She should have known. The signs were there, as clear as the glass window above the sink. His tenderness, his caring, his gentle strength. She recognized the signs because they mirrored her own feelings. Finally she could admit them. And they still scared the hell out of her.

"We thought it was a vacation fling." He laughed, but there was no humor in the sound.

Dani opened her eyes. "Yes."

He held her gaze. "It was never that for me."

"Hamp, I meant it when I said I would not let myself fall in love."

"I know. You were honest from the start."

"I was wrong."

It took a second. Then Hamp's eyes flared with deep emotion, a warm flame burning steadily there. Reaching out, he brought her against him, cradling her head against his chest. He let go of the breath he'd been holding. "Say it," he challenged softly.

"I love you, Hamp, but—"

"No, my darling, there are no buts to go with those words. Buts are for other sentences. Tell me again."

"I love you."

His hand tightened in her hair suddenly, briefly. "I love you." He bent his head, seeking her lips with a hunger like none he'd ever known—a reckless demand for intimacy. He broke off the kiss to bury his face in the soft skin of her neck. "Is David here?"

The question was like a face full of cold water. "Oh, Lord, yes. He's asleep."

Hamp forced down the desire that burned through him like a hot poker and let her go.

Her hands were shaking, she noticed as she took mugs from the cabinet.

He noticed, too, and caught her hand in his. He stared down at it for a minute. "You know, I can't stand to see you shake. It does something to me," he said hoarsely. He lifted her palm to his lips.

With her free hand Dani ran her fingers through his thick, sun-streaked hair. "Hamp, I meant it when I said 'I love you, but...'" She touched his lips. "We have to face the buts. All I can see are problems, real problems. We've known each other barely three weeks and these emotional ups and downs are draining both of us. Our argument last night was as much my fault as yours, but it was an awful experience. I don't want it to happen again. You have your classes; I have my business. We can't see each other without wanting more. And right now, unless you can figure out a way for one of us to be in two places at once, it's impossible."

Hamp picked up the coffee mug and filled it while he thought. He wanted more; he wanted it all, and he didn't believe it was impossible. But he'd just received the biggest concession, covered the biggest hurdle he had to face. The rest would come.

Maybe the best course of action *would* be to back off a little. But it might be the hardest thing he'd ever done. "You're right," he conceded. "I don't want a repeat of last night, either." He gave her a wry grin. "We've—I've—been approaching our situation from an emotional standpoint, when I should have been looking for a practical solution."

Dani told herself she wasn't disappointed. She'd asked for space and he was giving it to her. So why wasn't she happy? She forced lightness into her voice. "Gary has learned quickly. He did a good job while I was gone, so I'll be giving him more responsibility. When GG's baby gets well and she starts performing, I'll have more time."

"In the fall, when my regular classes begin again, I won't be teaching at night."

The fall? This was only the first of July. She hadn't asked for *that* much time. "I guess it's for the best," she said.

"You will plan to be at the party next week, won't you?"

Dani's spirits sank to another level. "I wouldn't miss it for the world."

9

ON SUNDAY AFTERNOON, a week later, Dani slipped her new dress over her head, enjoying the whisper of sound made by the fabric. She was unbearably excited at the prospect of seeing Hamp again. A week could seem like a year when you loved someone. Even longer when he loved you back.

The dress was a dream, she decided as she whirled in front of her mirror. Of heather silk, its cut and style looked like something out of the romantic fifties. A Sabrina neckline skimmed her collarbone and the bodice was tightly fitted and the skirt full, making her small waist look tiny. The sleeves, also fitted, ended just below the elbow. She slid her feet into very high-heeled pumps, sprayed on a mist of her favorite perfume and gave a last pat to her chignon. "David, are you ready?" she called.

"Ready," came the answer from the living room.

He smiled as she entered the room. "You look beautiful, Mom. I like your new dress."

Freshly shaved, with his dark hair combed neatly and dressed in his navy blue suit, white shirt and burgundy tie, David appeared older, more mature than his eighteen years. Dani felt a burst of pride as she studied him. "Thank you, honey. You look good, too," she said lovingly. "Shall we go?"

David had washed and polished her three-year-old Ford this morning and the metallic gray color gleamed like newly minted silver. He held the door for her before circling to take the driver's seat.

When they reached the highway that would take them north into Palo Alto proper, he glanced over to catch Dani moving her hands restlessly in her lap. "Are you nervous, Mom?" he asked.

"Not really." Before she had met Hamp, the prospect of spending an evening with a bunch of academians would have been a tedious one, not threatening her self-confidence, but ripe with the possibility of boredom. Now she was not nervous but uneasy. She admitted to herself that she wanted the people at this party to like her. She'd never felt this way in the past; she was what she was.

With the advent of Hamp Lowell a lot of things had changed in her life. She smiled and explained to David, "This party is a little bit like walking out onto a strange stage for the first time, not knowing your audience. But we'll have a good time." She would finally see Hamp in his own setting and meet his family, his friends and co-workers. The party might be interesting and it certainly wouldn't be dull.

"Don't worry. You'll do fine. Hamp said you'd fit in anywhere."

Surprised, she turned in her seat to look at him. When had they discussed her? Something was amiss here. "'Hamp said'? When did you talk to Hamp?"

"He dropped by the other night, to bring a book he thought I'd like to read. Didn't I tell you?"

"No." Dropped by? It was a forty-minute drive. How odd.

"He didn't stay long," David blurted, further mystifying her.

The only reason that came to mind to explain Hamp's visit sent her heart plummeting to her stomach. "David, is something the matter? Is it your scholarship?"

"My scholarship! No. Everything's fine. In fact I got a letter yesterday confirming the funds." He paused for a minute and then changed the subject. "It'll be good to see Sandy again. I've missed the little brat," he said affectionately. "But she'll probably come back with all sorts of New York opinions."

His surprise wasn't feigned. What then? She shrugged. As long as the scholarship was secure, she was content. And it was nice of Hamp to make the long drive to bring a book to David. "I've missed Sandy, too," she said.

Sandy's plane was to land at eight. It had been arranged that David would leave the party to meet her at the airport. Then he would drop her off at home and drive Dani back to their place.

Finally, following directions Hamp had given them, they were on the right street. "Here, David. It should be the next driveway," she said, looking for numbers on mailboxes set into stone pillars. Nothing as gauche as a name appeared on any of them.

Dani caught her breath at the sight of the magnificent Spanish-style house that was set back at least fifty yards from the street. "Good grief!"

"Boy, that's some house!" said David, awestruck.

Dani had expected a beautiful old home, but her imagination hadn't stretched this far. The center section was two stories, but on each side, angled wings extended like welcoming arms. The stucco was blindingly white. Red tiles scalloped the roof and a profusion of California ivy had been allowed to grow up the walls in places, softening the starkness. A wide circular drive followed the lines of the house.

As their car entered the drive, a woman in a starched gray uniform opened the door. Hamp must have been waiting nearby. He passed the woman and ran lightly down the steps to meet them. He was dressed, as he had been last Saturday night, in conservative black evening clothes and he looked magnificent. Dani remembered the stained cuffs and felt guilty. A man who lived in a house like this should never get his cuffs dirty.

A young man appeared from out of nowhere. "May I park your car for you, sir?"

"Certainly," said David with surprising aplomb. He handed the keys to the man.

"Hello, David," said Hamp, shooting her son a grin. Then he took Dani's hand with an odd tenderness. "Welcome," he said softly and kissed her, his mouth lingering for a longer moment than etiquette granted.

Her lips melted under his. Her hand went to his chest, her fingers straying underneath the lapels of his dinner jacket. He smelled clean and spicy—and wonderful.

When he raised his head, the expression in his dark eyes was soft, almost anxious. "I'm glad you came early. I want to show you around." He put her hand on his arm, rather formally, she thought, and covered it with his own in a firm grip, as though he didn't plan to let go for a long time.

With effort, Dani tore her gaze from his and fixed her attention on the shaded veranda that ran the length of the structure before her. "It's a beautiful house, Hamp."

Hamp admired it with her. He loved the house. "My grandfather built it in the twenties. When he died I was the only one who had any feeling for the place, so he left it to me. It's much too big, of course, but I can't bring myself to sell it." He led the way to the door where the uniformed woman waited, unabashed curiosity in her eyes. "Dani, this is Miranda. Miranda, Mrs. Fox and her son, David."

"How do you do, Miranda?" said Dani.

Miranda smiled broadly. "Mrs. Fox. I'm very pleased to meet you."

Dani glanced up at Hamp, wondering at the woman's enthusiasm, but he had escorted her out of the sunshine into the cool, dark foyer. It took a moment for her eyes to adjust to the dimmer light. On a table in the center of the hall stood a Flemish arrangement of Rubiosa lilies in a silver wine cooler. To her left she could see into a formal dining room with white tapers in candelabra, chafing dishes and serving trays, arranged and ready. Before them a curving staircase soared toward the second floor.

A second woman who seemed completely appropriate to this house was descending. She wasn't conventionally beautiful—*arresting* was a better word. "Regal" seemed the only description for her carriage. Her dress was black, and her black hair was swept back from her face into a severe twist. Dani had expected an older woman when Hamp mentioned his aunt, but this woman couldn't be forty. When she stepped off the last riser, Dani discovered that she was taller than she'd appeared at first—almost as tall as Hamp.

"Aunt Delores, I'd like for you to meet Danielle Fox. Dani, this is my aunt."

"Actually, I'm his great-aunt. How do you do, Danielle?" Dani's free hand was clasped in a firm grip. "And this must be David."

Dani reassessed her estimate of the woman's age as she neared, but his great-aunt? "Yes, may I present my son?" she said.

David shook hands with the woman, his response correct and polite. But there was a glimmer of amusement in his eyes that Dani didn't understand.

Hamp put a warm hand over Dani's. "Aunt Dee, would you find David something to drink? I want to show Dani the house before the guests arrive."

"Certainly, Hamp. Come along, David. I imagine you're hungry. We'll go into the kitchen and annoy the caterers."

"I think I'm in love," said David.

Dani frowned at the careless response, but she needn't have worried. Hamp's aunt laughed lightly. "In that case, we'll also plunder the refrigerator."

"Let's begin in the back," said Hamp, his words accompanied by what could only be a sigh of relief.

Dani smiled slightly.

He led the way to a dark-paneled study that looked out over a shimmering pool. A huge carved-mahogany desk dominated the room. When they were both inside, he closed the door. She turned, not surprised, and found his arms waiting to enfold her. It was like coming home after a long journey. "Oh, Hamp, I've missed you. Hold me."

"I was afraid you'd be late and I wouldn't have time...." His mouth covered hers and she responded to his hunger, welcoming the thrust of his tongue, burying her hands in his thick hair. He wasn't gentle; she didn't want him to be. They had this, she mused; this instant, totally satisfying hunger for each other. Though their meetings might be rare for the time being, at least they had this sensual awareness that exploded like the Fourth of July whenever they were near each other. She slid her hands under his jacket, around his waist, to feel his solid warmth through the thin material of his shirt. But that wasn't enough. With a soft sound she tugged the shirt free of his waistband. Her fingers roamed luxuriously over his muscular back.

Without releasing Dani's mouth, Hamp took a step back, feeling for a chair with his foot and collapsed into it, pulling her onto his lap, wrapping her in his arms. If he could only keep her here like this for the rest of his days, he would be in heaven on earth. His love for her had grown deeper, more profound, with separation; his desire for her was almost intolerable.

Her fingers on the skin of his back, the taste of her mouth, the exotic scent she wore, all went to his head like fine cognac, leaving him reeling. His hands moved over her shoulders, her breasts, down her thighs to the hem of her skirt. He paused at her knee, the fingers gripping hard in an attempt at control. He wanted her here, now, on the thin old rug at their feet.

Dani tasted his long, shuddering breath, his frustration, as he fought to curb his raging desire. Finally he broke off the kiss. His hand dropped to hang loosely at the side of the chair; his head rested against its leather-upholstered back. Closing his eyes he sighed deeply, heavily. "Dammit, Dani. I ought to resent the hell out of you for making me lose control every time I touch you. No other woman has ever had that effect on me."

Smiling tremulously and trying to slow her breathing, Dani let her head fall to his shoulder. She studied him in profile from a perspective that was impossible head-on because of his glasses. His strength was evident in the planes of his face, softened only by the heavy fringe of lashes against his cheek, and in the firm line of his lips, in the solid jaw. "I'm not exactly the picture of restraint around you, either."

His eyes remained shut, but the corners of his mouth lifted in a gratified smile. "No, you aren't, are you? That's what encourages me."

"I can't imagine why you need any more encouragement. It seems to me that I've more or less fallen in with all your suggestions so far." Her voice was not without irony.

He opened his eyes and looked down at her. His expression was suddenly serious. "Not all of them."

"All that were feasible, Hamp," she told him, softly sighing. "I became part of a holiday foursome when all I wanted to do was loaf, I went to Huahine on Jonny's rust-bucket plane, I fell in love with you when I'd told myself I absolutely would not."

Her words prompted memories that brought a smile back to Hamp's lips. "Dani—no, wait." Interrupting himself, he slid her off his lap and onto the chair. He crossed to the desk and opened the center drawer.

The leather under her was soft and gently aged, resilient. She curled her body, wanting to retain the warmth that Hamp had left there.

A knock sounded at the door to the hall.

Hamp bit off a curse. "What is it?" he asked the unseen person.

The soft voice of his aunt barely penetrated the door. "Hamp, the first car just entered the gates. I think it's Larry and Gina."

With a sigh of resignation he closed the drawer. "Thanks, Aunt Dee. We'll be right out," he called through the door.

Feeling a tinge of regret at the interruption, nevertheless Dani stood up, straightening the skirt of her dress, smiling a bit sadly.

"My brother and his wife," Hamp explained, coming to stand beside her.

The explanation was unnecessary, though he wasn't aware of that.

"Dani, I can't take a hell of a lot more of this," he informed her, scowling as he ran his hand through his hair.

"I'm beginning to feel the same way," she admitted. She reached up to smooth his hair where he'd rumpled it. Moving as of its own accord her hand touched his lapel, then his tie, straightening it, too. It was a proprietary action and uncharacteristic of her. "You'd better tuck your shirt in," she said quickly, to cover her reaction.

"Yes, ma'am." Hamp obeyed her direction, unable to hide his satisfied smile. He was fully conscious of the implications in her gesture. With a warm hand at her back he guided her to the door, opened it, and waited for her to precede him into the hall. "I have something to discuss with you after this party is over," he murmured under his breath. "And I'll wring the neck of the first person who tries to interrupt us." In a normal tone he said, "Honey, I want you to meet my sister-in-law and my brother."

I've met your brother, said Dani to herself, but not to him as she led the way toward the group by the front door. *Here it comes*, Dani said to herself, squaring her shoulders. She had expected this confrontation, had prepared herself for it and, in a way, relished it, since she'd learned that Hamp was a member of the newspaper family named Lowell.

She had avoided telling him that she knew his brother, because such an admission would lead to questions and an account of why and how. She had decided to wait and see how Larry Lowell reacted to their encounter.

The family resemblance wasn't strong, but looking at both men together, she could see that it was there. His brother had the same sun-streaked hair, the same dark eyes. But where Hamp's shone with intelligence, Larry's were smoky with suspicion and disbelief when he saw Dani approach at his brother's side. She wasn't surprised that the suspicion was directed at her.

Hamp's grandfather had established a chain of suburban newspapers from southern California to the Napa Valley. Hamp's brother had taken over the family businesses when Hamp had decided on an academic career. To say that the Lowells were a wealthy family was a gross understatement; Larry was probably suspicious of any woman his brother was seeing.

Dani maintained an expression of polite interest as Hamp introduced them.

Larry was a cool one. He responded to the introduction as though he had never met her, never heard of Danielle Fox or a supper club called Foxy's. His wife, Gina, was an airhead, but a good-natured airhead, Dani decided after only a few minutes of conversation.

The sounds of cars in the driveway ended the exchange with no blood drawn on either side.

Hamp could hardly bear to be separated from Dani. For the first hour he lingered nearby, neglecting his other guests, drinking in the sight of her, so stunning and unique. Her manner was effortless and he was fascinated by her effect on everyone in the room. Fascinated, that is—except for the effect on the unattached men. He caught a glimpse of himself in a mirror, frowning. He dismissed a jealous pang at the sound of her laughter and made himself join the guests on the patio.

Hamp's guests made a pleasant party, thought Dani a couple of hours later, wandering from group to group, fulfilling her hostess duties as Hamp had asked her to do. The curiosity concerning her presence that had permeated the atmosphere of the party with the arrival of the first guests, now had decreased noticeably. She wasn't unknown in the city, and she supposed it was natural for them to wonder.

For the first hour Hamp had hovered over her as though afraid to leave her side. Rather than being reassuring, his attentive presence had made her uncomfortable. Gradually he had begun to ease away, perhaps realizing that she was perfectly capable of handling herself. What did he expect, she thought nastily, that I would spit on the carpet? I do this kind of thing every night of my life.

The only thing that bothered her about the crowd was its size and trying to keep all the names and positions straight. There were well over a hundred people here, wandering through the living and dining rooms, spilling out onto the terrace around the pool. A few faces, regular patrons at her club, were easy to put names to, but the majority of the guests were strangers.

"Tired?" murmured Hamp from behind her. He put his hands on her shoulders and began a slow massage.

Dani glanced around, but no one seemed to be paying attention to them. She gave herself up to the manipulation of his strong fingers. "Umm. No. I'm not tired, but that feels good. Has David left?"

"About fifteen minutes ago. You're handling the party well."

"I'm enjoying myself. Tell me, Hamp, did you think I would embarrass you in front of your friends?" she said with mild reproach.

His hands clamped down hard and he spun her to face him, searching her face. "Where did you get such an idea? I was afraid you'd be bored stiff."

Dani's eyes fell shut as she realized how mistaken she had been about his motives. "Bored? Is that why you've been following me around like a bloodhound?"

"A bloodhound?" He chuckled. "Is that what I'm doing? No, I simply wanted to be as close to you as I could," he told her softly, watching for her reaction in the depths of her beautiful green eyes.

It was quick and sincere. "I misunderstood, Hamp. I'm sorry."

Squeezing her arms once more he kissed her forehead, his lips warm, then pulled her in under his arm. He looked around at the crowd—laughing, talking, drinking, eating—and wished them all to perdition.

"How often do you do this sort of thing?" she asked.

"Only a couple of times a year." Deliberately he dropped his voice an octave. "Most of the entertaining I do is on a much smaller scale. Modest dinner parties."

"Really? How modest?"

"Not too large," he said innocently, but his lips twitched. "Never more than thirty."

"I walked right into that one," Dani acceded wryly.

"I wish I could as easily walk you right into my bedroom upstairs."

Dangerous. This was so dangerous, but she felt the pull and she could no more resist it than she could stop her heartbeat. "Oh?" She lifted a brow and threw out the challenge with a smile. "And what would you do with me when you got me there?"

He proceeded to tell her, in explicit detail, throwing out a question occasionally to make sure she was on her toes. To anyone watching, his features showed polite interest and mild amusement, but his voice had settled to an intimate level. His gaze dropped to skim lightly over her curves.

Dani held her own, but the price was dear. The game was exciting, she had to admit—standing amid a crowd, engaging in a contest of sexual suggestion. She held her breath, expending a great amount of energy trying not to show how much influence he could bring to bear within a very short period of time. She schooled her features to the same polite mask he wore and exhaled in defeat. "Hamp, I believe one of your guests is trying to get your attention," she pointed out.

"Coward," he accused softly.

"To the bone," she conceded.

The laughter burst from him, startling a few people around them.

"Call out if you need me," he said. "And have something to eat."

Hamp left her with a small smile on her lips. She glanced up to see Larry making his way toward where she stood. Not overtly, it was a stop-and-go sort of progress, but she was definitely the prey. She stood where she was, waiting, but the smile had faded. There was going to be a confrontation; she'd known it from the first. No need to postpone the inevitable, which might be easier here in these social surroundings.

"Mrs. Fox—" he nodded, toasting her with his glass "—how's business?"

It was the wrong thing to say. His words served only to irritate her and emphasize the conflict between them. "Business is very brisk, Mr. Lowell. Better by far than it was two years ago. How's yours?"

"I was doing my civic duty, Ms Fox." he said smoothly.

"Trying to boost circulation, you mean. Do you think your grandfather would have approved of your muckraking tactics?" she asked, her demeanor equally unruffled.

His neck grew dangerously red. "Several of the clubs covered in the sheriff's investigation were found to harbor undesirable elements of criminal activity."

"Don't quote your own editorial to me, Mr. Lowell. I was just as glad to see those places close as you were, but publishing the list of every club within the county had the effect of tarring us all with the same brush, and you know it." She realized that her voice was climbing. She deliberately lowered it to a murmur. "Not an honorable thing to do at all. Not worthy of the type of journalism you claim to believe in. I thought the Lowell chain prided itself on setting an example of fairness for the rest of the press."

He opened his mouth to defend himself. Just then, one of the guests walked by, greeting them casually. As soon as he had passed, Dani turned away, afraid that she would go too far if the conversation resumed. She found herself brought up short against Hamp's broad chest.

Catching her hand in his, he looked from one of them to the other. "What's going on here?" he demanded.

She'd decided long ago that Hamp had no idea of the events of two years ago. He would have mentioned them long before this. "Nothing. Your brother and I were just renewing our acquaintance," she said calmly. All at once she was aware that several pairs of eyes were on them. Ashamed that she had let this man get to her, she laid a hand on Hamp's sleeve, feeling the strength of the tensed muscles there. "Really, Hamp. It's nothing. Is it, Larry?"

Larry searched her features for a moment. She saw again the suspicion in his eyes—and something else: disillusionment.

The expression puzzled her for a moment, then suddenly she remembered: during the investigation it had come out that one of his star reporters, a man who was also a close personal friend, was taking payoffs from the owners of some of the clubs. The facts, as they came to light, had embarrassed the papers and damaged their credibility.

How odd that she'd forgotten. At the time she'd gloated—while she tried to exist on dwindling profits. Now she tried not to feel sorry. Even though he was Hamp's brother, she didn't want to feel sympathy for this man.

"No," he finally agreed, relaxing and smiling slightly at something he saw in her eyes. "Nothing important." He glanced down at his watch. "Have you seen Gina, Hamp? We'd better be going." He turned to Dani. "I hope we'll have a chance to talk again soon, Mrs. Fox."

"I hope so, too." Her words were more than a platitude, she realized, surprised. Time had mellowed her more than she'd thought. "And please call me Dani." Maybe the resentment she had harbored in the past toward this man would someday fade. He was, after all, Hamp's brother.

"Dani," Larry acknowledged. "Good night, Hamp."

Hamp didn't question her further, for the party had begun to break up. As he had said they would, a few stragglers lingered. Aunt Dee had left with another couple who were going to drop her at her home. Finally, at nine-thirty, Hamp closed the door on the last of the guests. "I'll tell

Miranda she can go, and pay off the caterers. Meet me in the study."

"Okay." Dani shed her high-heeled pumps as soon as she entered the room. She breathed a sigh of relief and sank onto the couch, folding her legs under her.

Hamp came into the room a few minutes later. He crossed to the desk and picked up a cut-glass decanter. "Brandy?" he asked, glancing over his shoulder. When she shook her head he turned back to pour himself one.

Dani raked her hand through her hair, forgetting that it was arranged in a chignon. The action loosened some of the pins so she took them all out and shook her hair free, letting it fall over her shoulders. "I wonder where David and Sandy are."

Hamp watched her shake her hair. He backed up to the desk, half sitting against the edge. "Miranda told me he'd called from the airport to say Sandy's plane was late." He looked at his watch. "She should be landing about now. What was all that between you and Larry?" he asked.

Dani related the story, a shortened version. The man had put her through hell; some of it, he'd never know about.

When her place of business was listed with others of dubious honesty, there had been certain elements that wanted to move in, whether they believed the stories were true or not. She'd hired one or two unsavory characters before she discovered her mistake. They'd been easier to hire than to fire.

Hamp swore, long and creatively, when she finished. "Two years ago? I spent most of the summer in Australia, teaching a course there. I didn't know a damned thing about this, Dani. I swear I didn't."

She was confused. "You aren't involved with the paper."

"Except that I sit on its board of directors. When I have to be out of the country for any length of time Larry usually catches me up on what's been happening." He studied her over the rim of his glass for a reaction.

The information surprised her; she hadn't known of his connection. Even so—she studied his features slowly, one by one. "I knew you weren't aware of the situation, Hamp," she stated firmly.

Hamp's heart did a somersault. If she had finally let down that last barrier to intimacy, it was going to make his plans much easier. "Trust, Dani?" he asked very softly.

She looked away from that dark, piercing gaze. There was an intensity in him tonight, a purposefulness she didn't understand. Running a fingernail along the welting of the sofa arm, she thought for a minute. "Yes, and the fact that, had you known, you would have mentioned it."

"I wonder why Larry didn't tell me about the investigation," he speculated, playing for time as he circled to the desk. He opened the center drawer.

"Probably because he was embarrassed," she said sharply. She explained about the aborted crusade and the reporter's part in it.

He closed the desk drawer with more force than the venerable piece deserved. "You should have sued," he said flatly.

"I almost did, but in the end I was just glad to have it over."

Hamp slid his hand into the pocket of his jacket and drained the brandy glass, thinking about all she'd told him. His anger at his brother would have taken on greater significance if he hadn't had other, more vital, things on his mind. "Tell me, did you enjoy the party?" he asked, coming over to join her on the sofa.

If Dani was surprised at the switch in the conversation, she didn't show it. She was relieved that the subject was behind them. Determination had helped her put it out of her mind two years ago and she had taken no pleasure in the re-hashing tonight. She half turned to face him and chuckled. "I enjoyed the party very much. Thank you for asking me."

Reaching for her hand he linked their fingers and brought them to his lap, tugging her closer. He smiled into her up-turned face. "Very proper, Ms Fox," he said. "From your expression I gather you didn't expect to."

"Well—" she hedged "—a formal party really isn't my kind of thing."

"Do you think you could put up with hostessing once or twice a year?" he asked.

She rubbed her cheek on his sleeve, like a kitten seeking warmth. "Ask me six months from now."

"I'm asking you now."

His tone of voice warned her. She was suddenly still. "Hamp . . ."

His fingers tightened on hers, gripping them almost painfully. "I have something—ah—Dani, do you— Hell! I'm doing this badly. Dani, will you marry me?"

She would have laughed at the imperturbable profes-sor's awkwardness had the predicament not been so grave. As it was, she suddenly wanted to cry. Her eyes fastened onto his dark gaze. She shook her head, stunned.

Why hadn't she been prepared for this? she asked herself wildly. She should have been. Growing from thoughts of love, thoughts of marriage were normal. At least they were for most people. Not for her.

Hamp knew from Dani's expression that she was going to say no and it was going to hurt like hell. He felt the des-peration build inside him. And the helplessness. But his face didn't betray his feelings. He couldn't afford to let it. "Be-fore you answer, darling, let me tell you that David knows that I was going to ask you to marry me. He approves."

Dani shook her head, but she couldn't seem to shake the untidiness in her brain that kept her from thinking straight. She put a hand to her temple. "You talked to David before you talked to me?"

"David and I are friends, Dani, and he is your son. I knew you wouldn't accept my proposal without first considering him. And I didn't want to be the cause of any resentment between the two of you."

"Hamp, we've known each other for only slightly over a month. This is not something we can decide so quickly."

"Does love have to fit into a timetable, Dani?" he asked softly, very softly. "Do we waste weeks, months of our lives, while we wait for the time to be right?" His expression was inscrutable, but she could feel his rigidity through his fingers. "We know each other better than some of the married couples here tonight. Try again."

Dani disengaged their hands and stood. Crossing her arms over her racing heart, she paced the length of the room and back. "I can't picture myself as the wife of a college professor."

Hamp plunged his hands into his pockets and slid down on the sofa until he was resting on his spine. His chin sank into his shirtfront. "That's better, but no gold star. I had never imagined myself married to a nightclub singer, either, but I found a woman who could give me the joy I thought was lost with my youth, and I've fallen deeply in love with her."

Though he wasn't looking at her, the declaration was simple and clear and honest. Dani turned away, squeezing her eyes shut, knowing the price of his admission. He was used to keeping his emotions inside, well under control. He'd known the pain of desertion once. He'd vowed it wouldn't happen again, just as she had; but unlike Hamp, she was not willing to take a chance again.

The past two weeks had shown her too much. Their lives were too diverse to meld. They would end up pulling, tearing each other apart. "Hamp, I'm sure you think you mean that, but you'll regret it. I'm not right for you."

Suddenly, angrily, he came up off the sofa to grasp her shoulders from behind, giving her a little shake. "What the hell are you talking about? You're exactly right for me."

She raised a hand to cover one of his as she tried to keep the reasonableness in her voice. "Hamp, I'm trying to be reasonable for both of us. You know how much time we've had together since we've been home."

"Why the hell do you think I'm asking you to marry me? The situation as it is now is intolerable." His angry tone left no doubt that he meant it.

Turning to face him, she said placatingly, "I know, I know. But it would be worse if we were married. You don't like it when I have to work until four in the morning—"

Harshly he interrupted, "I love you, Dani; those things can be worked out."

At whose expense? she asked herself as she searched his features. But the damage was done; his expression was closed to her.

"I've just asked you to marry me. Will you?"

"No. I can't. I'm sorry."

Hamp stared at the beautiful woman he loved so much and wondered if his heart would ever assume its normal rhythm again. "Do you know what the real problem is?" he mused, almost to himself. His voice sounded harsh and strange to his ears. "You're afraid."

Her chin rose a notch. "I'm not afraid of anything," she responded automatically; which was, of course, not true.

"Aside from stage fright and a fear of flying," he began dryly, his gaze boring into hers, "you're also afraid to give up your independence. You're afraid of the risk; afraid to trust unless the trusting doesn't cost you anything. From the very first, as soon as I moved in close, you withdrew."

Never had she wanted to rip away his glasses more than she did at that moment. They were like a wall between them, giving him a protection, an advantage she didn't have.

"Marrying me, meshing your life with mine, wouldn't be easy, we both know that," he went on. "But I misread your capacity for courage, Dani, and for happiness. And I feel sorry for both of us."

His words were delivered like tiny buckshot, each one leaving a wound. They added to the chaos that was her brain. *Was* she a coward? *Was* she clinging to her independence at the cost of her happiness?

"I think I hear a car." Leaving her standing in the middle of the room, he crossed to the door and opened it. "By the way, I talked with Sandy as well as David." His mouth twisted. "They knew I was going to propose to you tonight; they were delighted. I'll leave it to you to explain to David why you turned me down." He hesitated on his way out. "And I promise he won't suffer for your decision."

HOURS LATER Dani lay on her bed, her body stiff and aching. She reflected on the reaction of the teenagers to their announcement that there would be no marriage. The smile of pleasure on her son's face had faded to one of confusion and disappointment. And Sandy had picked up a cat that had appeared from nowhere and buried her face there as she fled upstairs.

Patiently Dani had tried to explain her reasons to David on the way home, but she might as well have saved her breath. He asked only one question: Did she love Hamp? She admitted that she did, very much. After that he gave only mumbled responses and she had an idea he didn't hear another word she said.

She was strong; she would get over this. She had done the right thing. Every ridiculous cliché she'd ever scorned didn't help. Not until she felt moisture seep into her hair at the temples, did she realize that she was crying.

HAMP LOCKED the front door behind them and picked up Sandy's overnight case along with his own. "Let's go," he said with deceptive animation.

"Wait." Sandy stopped him with a hand on his arm, her head cocked in a listening position. "Was that the phone?"

Hamp paused, listening, hope dying hard in him. He'd given Miranda the weekend off, so she wasn't there to answer. But all he heard was the sound of traffic. "I don't hear anything, sweetheart." He stored the suitcases in the trunk and got into the car beside her.

He had decided on the spur of the moment last night to take Sandy to the coast for a day and night. Anything to get out of the house.

The effects of all this on his daughter had angered him. Certainly he wouldn't have wanted Dani to marry him for the sake of either of the children, but dammit, couldn't she see what she was doing to all of them? At least Sandy and David had remained friends. He'd come in several times to find David there, acting oddly embarrassed. And that angered him, too.

Tomorrow it would be two weeks.

Now he knew it was all over; now he knew she'd really meant it. *What did you expect?* he asked himself, as he pulled onto the highway. *You went into this with your eyes wide open. You've been deserted before. You knew the risks of opening your heart.* With Dani he'd been willing to take the chance.

The way to hold Dani was not to try to hold her. She had to make the first move if there was to be anything between them again. But, Lord, he'd missed her. During the first week he'd lived with the expectation of hearing from her any minute. She loved him; she'd call, he'd told himself a hundred, a thousand times. But she hadn't. When days passed without a call, he'd begun to despair that he'd ever hear from her again.

Now he knew he would not.

Never had his life seemed so empty.

DANI PICKED up the telephone again. Her hand trembled with the effort as though the receiver weighed a ton. With a rosy-tipped nail she punched in Hamp's telephone number. She listened to the ring and listened. Finally she hung up. It had been almost two weeks since the debacle at Hamp's house. Two interminable weeks tomorrow.

She had suffered through the first week—the pain of loss a heavy burden, like death, that had to be endured. The second week had begun in anger—why had he *done* this to her?—which had quickly dissolved to—why had she done this to him? The relationship between them had built too suddenly, but was that any reason to deny its depth?

Hamp had accused her of being afraid. After much soul-searching she was finally able to admit the truth of his accusation. Her life had been comfortable as it was. She had been frightened of changing all that, of trusting her happiness to another.

Only when she was able to admit her fear openly to herself could she see that her life also lacked a lot of essentials, such as sharing and tenderness and passion.

The rest of the days had been spent trying to get her thoughts and emotions into some kind of order. She had to call him, she knew that, but she didn't know what she was going to say.

She tried again, and each time her heart seemed to shrink in her chest. Finally she had to leave for the club. It was Saturday night at Foxy's. For some it had become a tradition; for herself, this Saturday was a chore.

The next afternoon she tried again. When the receiver was picked up, she began to smile, only to have her spirits plunge when she recognized Miranda's voice. "Lowell residence," said the housekeeper.

"Miranda, this is Danielle Fox. May I speak to Mr. Lowell, please?"

"Mr. Lowell is out of town, Mrs. Fox."

"Is he—are—" Damn! "When do you expect him back?"

"Tonight, sometime. I'm not sure exactly when. Shall I tell him you called?"

She would tell him anyway, thought Dani. "Yes, please," she said. "I'll call back."

"HAMP, THIS IS DANI. I hope I'm not calling too late."

On the other end of the connection Hamp gripped the receiver like a lifeline and shut his eyes. "Not at all. How are you?" he asked calmly.

"I'm fine. I wondered if you and Sandy would like to be my guests for dinner at the club this Wednesday. I've engaged a new jazz group out of Kansas City for one night's performance, and I thought you might enjoy it."

Hamp smiled to himself, for the first time in two long, miserable weeks. When Miranda had told him of her phone call his first instinct was to drive immediately to Dani's apartment, sweep her into his arms, into his heart, and never let go.

But that tactic wouldn't work with her. He'd have to tread carefully. "I'd like that very much," he said. He paused. "I'm not sure about Sandy."

Dani caught her bottom lip between her teeth. She reasoned that the child hadn't forgiven her. "Tell her—tell her I'd love to have her if she can make it."

"I will."

"One other thing . . ." She gnawed at her lip again. "I've been having some trouble with my car and it's in the garage. I wonder if you'd mind picking me up? About eight?"

She was nervous. Hamp let out the breath he'd been holding, the tension melting from his rigid muscles like a snowball on a hot stove. His hope was reborn. "I'll be there," he said in a low voice, full of promise. He wondered how the hell he would last until Wednesday.

A few seconds later he went to search for his daughter.

"Come in," Sandy said when he knocked on her bedroom door.

She was propped up in bed with a book. "Hi, Daddy."

"Ready for bed?" He sat at the foot of a chaise longue, reluctant to begin this conversation. Sandy had reacted predictably at what she saw as Dani's rejection of them both. In the two weeks since the party he'd seen her both hurt and defiant when any remark was made that reminded her of Dani.

"Sandy, Dani has invited us to the club on Wednesday for dinner. Would you like to go?"

Her expression closed at the mention of Dani's name. "Wednesday?" she said emotionlessly, looking away. "Well, I've sort of made plans."

Which meant she would make some, he guessed from her expression. But he didn't say anything. He merely nodded. "Okay." He rose, slapping his jeans-clad thigh.

"Don't go over there, Daddy," she said suddenly. "You don't have to put yourself through this. There are a lot of women who would marry you in a minute."

He might never get this opportunity again so he sat back down, this time on the edge of her bed, and reached for her hand. "Honey, I don't want to marry any other woman. Love doesn't work that way."

"How could you love her when she's put you through this?" she scoffed.

"She's afraid, honey. And she loves me, too."

She didn't accept that explanation, either. "What's she got to be afraid of? We're not monsters."

"No, she's not afraid of us. She's afraid of herself." He searched for the right words. "Dani's parents died when she was very young. Her grandparents brought her up, but they were older, and they died, too, when she was only eighteen. Then she lost her husband. Can you imagine yourself, not much older than you are right now, having lost so much, with a baby for whom you were totally responsible, and almost no money?"

Sandy considered it for a long time. "No, I guess not. When Mother died, I knew I had you. And my grandparents, and Uncle Larry and Aunt Dee."

"Dani didn't have anyone. She had to go to work when most kids are going to college. She never had those carefree days. She's worked like a little demon and been successful, but she's afraid to depend on someone else too much because she remembers too clearly what it's like to lose them."

Sandy relented slightly. "I feel sorry for her but . . ."

"No, you mustn't feel sorry. Pity is the last thing she would want. She's a proud woman."

"Are you sure she wants you back?"

He smiled. "I wish I *were* sure. I know she loves me. But I think she's making the overture because she can't stand this constraint between us. We had a good time together in the islands. I think she wants to remain friends."

Her lower lip thrust out stubbornly. "Could you be friends with someone who hurt you like that?"

"I don't know," he answered honestly.

"But you're going."

"Yes, I'm going."

"Well, I'm not," she announced in a tone that told him she thought he was a fool. He wondered himself, but he only knew that if there was a chance of breaking through Dani's barrier of self-protection, he had to try.

DANI FELT as though she was dressing for her funeral and she looked like it, too. The colorless linen skirt and blouse were things she wore often, but never together. She seized a bright aquamarine scarf and knotted it under her collar.

When she had asked David to join them for dinner, he'd told her in no uncertain terms how senseless this invitation was. He wanted no part of it. He'd also quoted Sandy on the state of her father's resentment until Dani wondered why Hamp had accepted.

The doorbell rang. Dani wiped damp palms on her linen skirt and went to answer it. Her smile wavered at the sight of him standing there, so tall and devastatingly handsome. "Hi. Come in," she said, taking a step back.

Hamp smiled, too, drinking in the sight of her. "Hi." He was gratified to see that his love was nervous, as if she'd just bailed out of a plane without a parachute.

"Would you like a drink before we go? I have Scotch."

"Fine." She disappeared into the kitchen while he settled himself on the living-room couch. The place was immaculate. His smile widened.

"Here's your drink," she told him cheerfully. As she handed him the glass, the ice rattled against the sides.

It was another encouraging sign.

"Cheers," she said, raising her wine goblet in salute. She sat in a chair across from him and took a short sip. "I'm sorry the kids couldn't be with us tonight."

Hamp let a long, pregnant silence stretch between them before he answered. "I'm not. This is between us, Dani. And it needs to be settled."

She didn't pretend to misunderstand. "Yes," she agreed. Shifting restlessly in her chair, she sipped her wine. He wasn't even going to give her the evening to get used to being with him again. She couldn't blame him. Sunday when they'd talked, she should have begged him to come over immediately. The intervening days had only increased her anxiety.

But tonight, if the evening went well, if Hamp still wanted to marry her, she would accept with joy and happiness and hope. As he'd said, meshing their life-styles wouldn't be easy, but she was determined to try if he was still willing.

Hamp stared down into his glass for a minute. When he raised his gaze again she caught her breath. "Why did you ask me here tonight?" he asked softly.

"Why? I thought..." She broke off, unable to endure that piercing gaze for a moment longer. She inhaled and blew the air out through pursed lips. Her head fell back against the chair. "Oh, Lord, Hamp, you know why." Her voice was so muted that she barely heard the words herself. "I just wish I hadn't waited three days."

Suddenly he was there, taking her goblet from nerveless fingers and setting it with his on the table beside her. He placed his hands on the arms of her chair, effectively imprisoning her. His eyes blazed hot and dark. "I want to hear you say it," he demanded. "After putting me through hell for two weeks and three days, I *have* to."

She removed his glasses and tossed them to the table. Her arms wound around his neck, pulling him down to her, blindly seeking his mouth. He allowed a certain distance, but didn't close the last few inches. She knew she would have to say the words if she wanted him to kiss her. She said them without hesitation, willingly, eagerly. They spilled out like golden sunlight from behind a rain cloud.

"I love you, I've missed you horribly, I was wrong. My life is empty without you in it—"

That wasn't everything that needed to be said, but it was enough for now. His mouth came crashing down, bruising her lips. He lifted her bodily from the chair, crushing her to him as though he'd never let go.

Dani led the way to the bedroom.

LATER THEY LAY facing each other, tangled in the sheets of Dani's bed, hovering somewhere between consciousness and dreaming, neither of them wanting to lose, in sleep, the wonderful feeling of completion. She neither quite trusted the certainty that he was real, nor that he wouldn't disappear like a dream if she slept.

The telephone rang. She sat straight up in bed and looked at the clock. Midnight. David. He was spending the night with a friend. She snatched up the receiver.

"Hello."

"Dani, this is Sandy."

Hamp switched on the light beside the bed. She put out a hand to him and he grasped it tightly.

"Yes, Sandy? Is something wrong, honey?"

Sandy! She had gone to a movie with Rocky Two. His first impulse was to grab the telephone, but he restrained himself.

Dani put the receiver between them.

"May I speak to David?"

The child was frightened. It would do no good to let Sandy know she was frightened, too. "David isn't here, honey; but I'll help you."

"I can't find my daddy, either," Sandy said in a rush, explaining more than she knew. "I know he was with you earlier." She wouldn't have called Dani except when she couldn't reach anyone else. On the other hand she could have called her uncle. So Dani wasn't *quite* a last resort.

But her voice was stiff as she explained, "I went to a movie with Rocky tonight. Afterward we came to a party some friends of his were having. He's had too much to drink; they all have. My curfew is past, and Daddy'll be mad if I don't get home. I could call a taxi, but . . ."

"We'll come for you right now." She hesitated, glancing at Hamp. "Your daddy is with me."

She heard the gasp before Hamp took the phone. "Sandy, you did the right thing, honey. Now don't be afraid, just tell me where you are."

Dani was already pulling on a pair of jeans by the time Hamp got the directions straight from the hysterical child. She threw his pants at him. "Hurry," she urged.

"Dani, my love, I need my glasses almost as much as I need my pants. Would you get them for me?"

"The place isn't far from here," he said as they raced across the lawn toward his car.

As he drove, she watched his hard-featured expression in profile. "Sandy hasn't forgiven me, has she?" she asked quietly.

He shot her a grimace. "No," he admitted. "She was pretty upset by our breakup."

"I've made so many problems for us."

He reached for her hand. Linking their fingers, he held it hard. "Not any problems that we can't solve together," he said firmly. "We do intend to be together, don't we?"

"Yes," she whispered immediately, covering his hand with hers. "Yes," she repeated in a stronger voice. "We do indeed intend to be together."

The party was spilling onto the lawn of the small house by the time they arrived. Sandy waited for them in the shadows of a tree. When she saw the car she started running. Hamp slammed on the brakes, jumped out and met her halfway. The child ran straight into his arms.

Dani stepped out onto the pavement, but waited for them to join her, unsure of her welcome.

His expression was grim as he handed the weeping child over to Dani. "Get her in the car. I'll be right back." He headed for the house, his long strides eating up the distance.

To Dani's relief, Sandy came into her embrace without hesitation, as naturally as though she belonged there. Dani squeezed her eyes shut, emotion distorting her features. "It's all right. You're all right now," she murmured over and over, as much to herself as to Sandy.

Hamp was back in a few minutes. Dani looked at him questioningly.

"I think I convinced them to break it up before the police arrived."

Surprised, Dani scanned the neighborhood. For the first time she noticed that lights were on in houses up and down the block.

Hamp grinned as he bundled them into the car. "Let's get out of here. I don't particularly relish having to explain my presence, either." He put the car in gear and headed back to Dani's apartment.

Safe between them, Sandy breathed in tiny spasms. The warmth from the young girl nestled under her arm afforded Dani a wonderful feeling of relief and completion.

Sandy recovered enough to intercept the melting smile she gave Hamp. "Have you and Dani made up?"

"Yes, sweetheart," said Hamp.

"You'll argue," she warned.

He smiled at Dani. "Maybe, but I prefer to think of it as disagreeing. And it doesn't mean we love each other, or you, any less." He hesitated. "Most married people disagree."

"You're going to get married?" Her voice rose on the last word.

Hamp laughed, a light youthful sound that made Dani's heart swell with love. "Tomorrow, if I can arrange it."

Sandy was quiet for a long minute. Dani held her breath. Then Sandy giggled. "Such unseemly haste, Professor," she said in a very adult way.

There was only one thing missing, and Hamp rectified that as soon as they were inside. "Where is David?" he said, striding toward the phone.

"He's sleeping over at a friend's house. Hamp, you can't call at this time of night," she protested. "It's almost one o'clock."

"Yes, I can," he answered firmly. "We're going to be a family, and the foursome isn't complete yet. I don't intend to let another hour go by before it is. What's the telephone number?"

"A family," said Sandy with satisfaction. Then she groaned aloud and flopped down on Dani's sofa. "That means I'll have to put up with a bossy brother," she complained. But her eyes gleamed merrily. She linked her fingers behind her head. "Maybe I'll take him to New York."

Dani laughed helplessly, but her eyes were damp with emotion. Hamp held out his arm and she moved to him, watched his features lovingly while he punched the number. He swiveled the mouthpiece of the telephone under his chin and covered her lips with a warm kiss.

"We'll argue." She repeated Sandy's warning, smiling against his mouth.

Hamp nodded, raising his head to look down into her beautiful green eyes. "It won't be peaceful, but it will be heaven." He brought the mouthpiece back up between them. "David . . . ?"

Harlequin Temptation

COMING NEXT MONTH

#213 A MAN LIKE DAVID Phyllis Roberts

Advertising for a fiancé was a risky venture, Holly knew, but she desperately needed a husband-to-be for the weekend. She hadn't dared hope that her ad would be answered by a man like David....

#214 BUILDING ON DREAMS Shirley Larson

Diana Powell wore a hard hat every day on the job—but she was far from being a hard-hearted woman. In fact, she had a real soft spot for Drew Lindstrom. Now if he would only let himself forget blueprints long enough to succumb to her...

#215 SPEAK TO THE WIND Mary Tate Engels

When Marla Eden was approached to work with Joe Quintero to help him hone his communications skills, she couldn't say no. After all, who could resist the handsome Apache leader? Little did she know that one day she'd need a helping hand in return....

#216 WHEN TOMORROW COMES
Regan Forest

Kyle and Margie were bound to be more than just good neighbors. They had *so* much in common...including the man who wanted to expose their scandalous pasts.

 *Harlequin American Romance.*

JOIN THE CELEBRATION!
THE FIFTH ANNIVERSARY
OF HARLEQUIN
AMERICAN ROMANCE

1988 is a banner year for Harlequin American
Romance—it marks our fifth anniversary.

For five successful years we've been bringing you
heartwarming, exciting romances, but we're not
stopping there. In August, 1988, we've got an
extraspecial treat for you. Join us next month when we
feature four of American Romance's best—and four
favorite—authors.

Judith Arnold, Rebecca Flanders, Beverly Sommers
and Anne Stuart will enchant you with the stories of
four women friends who lived in the same New York
apartment building and whose lives, one by one, take an
unexpected turn. Meet Abbie, Jaime, Suzanne and
Marielle—the women of YORKTOWN TOWERS.

Four believable American Romance heroines...four
contemporary American women just like you...by four
of your favorite American Romance authors.

Don't miss these special stories.
Enjoy the fifth-anniversary
celebration of Harlequin
American Romance!

HAR5-1

Temptation™

TEMPTATION WILL BE EVEN HARDER TO RESIST...

In September, Temptation is presenting a sophisticated new face to the world. A fresh look that truly brings Harlequin's most intimate romances into focus.

What's more, all-time favorite authors Barbara Delinsky, Rita Clay Estrada, Jayne Ann Krentz and Vicki Lewis Thompson will join forces to help us celebrate. The result? A very special quartet of Temptations...

- **Four striking covers**
- **Four stellar authors**
- **Four sensual love stories**
- **Four variations on one spellbinding theme**

All in one great month! Give in to Temptation in September.

TDESIGN-1

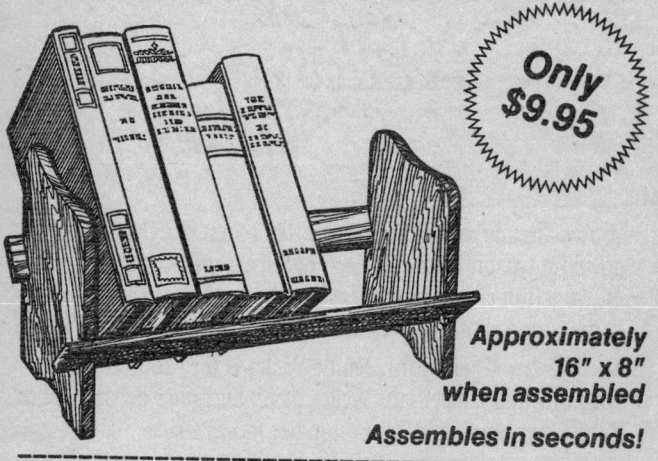

Lynda Ward's

LEAP THE MOON

...the continuing saga of *The Welles Family*

You've already met Elaine Welles, the oldest daughter of powerful tycoon Burton Welles, in Superromance #317, *Race the Sun*. You cheered her on as she threw off the shackles of her heritage and won the love of her life, Ruy de Areias.

Now it's her sister's turn. Jennie Welles is the drop-dead-gorgeous, most rebellious Welles sister, and she's determined to live life her way—and flaunt it in her father's face.

When she meets Griffin Stark, however, she learns there's more to life than glamour and independence. She learns about kindness, compassion and sharing. One nagging question remains: is she good enough for a man like Griffin? Her father certainly doesn't think so....

Leap the Moon...a Harlequin Superromance coming to you in August. Don't miss it!

LYNDA-1B